Rodeo Ashes

Shannon Taylor Vannatter

Heartsong Presents

To my awesome critique group—
Brenda Anderson, Jerri Ledford, and Lorna Seilstad.
Without your support, input, and suggestions, my editors would
have their work cut out for them. Thanks for putting up with my
first drafts and helping me hone them into something readable.

I appreciate DeeDee Barker-Wix, director of sales at the
Cowtown Coliseum, for answering countless rodeo-Stockyards questions.
Nancy Trammel-Downes, Aubrey City Hall secretary, and Deborah Goin,
Aubrey Main Street Committee member, helped with information about
Aubrey. Steve and Krys Murray, owners of Moms on Main, let me use
their restaurant in the books and allowed me to have a signing there
when I finally got to visit. I appreciate everyone in Aubrey, Texas,
for embracing me as one of their own.

A note from the Author:

I love to hear from my readers! You may correspond with me by writing:

Shannon Taylor Vannatter
Author Relations
P.O. Box 9048
Buffalo, NY 14240-9048

ISBN-13: 978-0-373-48629-8

RODEO ASHES

This edition issued by special arrangement with Barbour Publishing, Inc.,
1810 Barbour Drive, Uhrichsville, Ohio, U.S.A.

Chapter 1

"How did I fall for this?" Lacie Gentry squeezed the steering wheel of her parked SUV until her fingers went numb. "Because I'm the biggest idiot in Texas. And to top things off—I'm talking to myself."

Movement at the curb in front of her car, and strains of a cry-in-your-beer country song twanged out the open bar door. Please let it be her friends, ready to head home. She looked up into the leer of a man.

Oh goodness, what if he comes over here? Without taking her eyes off him, she found the lock button. The loud click broke the spell, and he turned away.

Her breath released in a huff.

She couldn't stay here like a sitting duck, waiting for some carjacker. Or worse. She'd never heard of anything good happening inside or outside a bar. Maybe she could go somewhere else and wait. But if she did, how would her *friends* find her when they got done with whatever they were doing in there?

She waited until the man drove away, scanned the Fort

Worth parking lot three times, unlocked the door, and bolted to the bar. The August night air hadn't cooled one iota, but a chill moved through her.

Safer inside or out? At least there were witnesses inside. She scurried into the bar as if wolves waited in the shadows.

But the wolves were inside.

A dishwater-blond man swaggered over to her. "Hey beautiful, I lost my phone number. Can I borrow yours?"

She sidestepped him and searched for a quiet corner.

One of her friends had plastered herself against a man in a booth. Big-time public display of affection. Lacie averted her eyes and spotted a corner. She hurried to the table.

No one notice me. No one notice me. No one notice me.

She scanned the bar for her other friend. There on the dance floor with a man—if you could call that dancing. Lacie's hand flew to her heart. What had she been thinking, getting in the car with these two? That they were grown women with sense and decency now? Wrong.

A painfully skinny man stumbled in her direction. She looked down at the table in front of her.

"Hey baby, I hope you know CPR, 'cause you take my breath away!" He leaned close enough for her to smell the liquor on his breath.

"Excuse me." She inched past him, searching frantically for an escape.

A neon sign proclaimed Gals, and she ran for the safety of the ladies' room.

The door swung closed, and she surveyed the dingy bathroom.

A denim-clad woman swayed to the country music as she stood at the sink applying lipstick. She missed her mouth, giggled, and tried again.

Lacie found a clean, empty stall. *Lord, if You'll get me out of here safely, I'll never be so stupid again.* She dug her cell phone from her pocket.

She couldn't call her sister. Star would tell Mama. And Mama had told her never, ever, ever step foot in a bar. She never had. Until now. Twenty-seven years old and her first time in a bar.

She grabbed a wad of toilet paper, shut the toilet lid, covered it with three paper liners, and then sat.

Call Rayna and Clay? Lacie would never hear the end of it. Her friends already thought her too trusting and naive. They didn't need any more ammo to convince her to move.

No choice. Just wait it out. Besides, even though Marcy and Geena hadn't acted as friends, Lacie couldn't leave them here without a ride home.

Rayna and Clay would ask questions if she came in really late, but she'd come up with something, and Max was fine with them.

Half the time she still thought of her son as Little Mel, even though she'd changed his nickname to Max over a year ago.

The door opened, followed by a moan. High-heel-clad feet stumbled to the stall next to Lacie. Heaving and splashing liquid. A foul odor emanated.

Lacie's stomach lurched. Covering her nose and mouth with one hand, she wrenched the door open and bolted for the exit.

She ran into something solid then stepped back away from the wobbly man. "I'm sorry. I wasn't watching where I was going."

"That's all right, darlin'. Can you give me directions?"

"To where?"

"To your heart."

Lacie rolled her eyes and blew out a big breath. Hmm... drunk guy or hurling woman in the bathroom?

"Here's your Coke, sweetheart." A man's deep voice, over her right shoulder. A calloused hand clamped on her elbow. "I found us a table right over here."

She spun around to give him a piece of her mind and met celery-colored eyes from her past. Quinn Remington.

"Sorry man"—the drunk splayed both hands up in the air—"I didn't know she was with someone." Then he slunk away.

Quinn tucked her hand in the crook of his elbow and steered her to an empty booth.

Sweetheart? They'd gone to high school together but never come close to dating. And she hadn't seen him since graduation. They definitely weren't on sweetheart terms, much less touching terms.

Besides, she was a widow. She pulled her arm away from him.

"Relax, Lacie. I'm not making any moves, just trying to rescue you. Unless you're interested in that guy."

"Oh. Definitely not." Heat warmed her face. "Thank you."

"I get the feeling you're not exactly comfortable here."

She scrambled to the safety of the booth he'd found for her. "I've never…never been in a bar before."

Quinn slid in on the vinyl seat across from her. His black coffee-colored hair contrasted with his pale eyes.

His eyebrows rose. "Never?"

"Well I've been to restaurants with bars in them, but never to a plain ol' bar before."

"I wish I could say the same."

As far as she knew, he'd never done the party scene in high school and hadn't been a drinker. She'd never pegged him as the type to hang out in a bar. But his eyes were different than she remembered. Haunted, as if pain dwelt there. "If you don't like bars, then why are you here?"

"Looking for one of my ranch hands."

Her parched lips longed to taste her cola, but what else was in it? Not that she didn't trust Quinn, but he might think mixed drinks were the norm. "Is he here?"

"Not so far." He scanned the crowd. "He's a great guy, a

hard worker, but an alcoholic who hasn't admitted he has a problem yet. He told me he went to one AA meeting, and I agreed to be his accountability partner."

"That's sad, but it's good of you to try to help him. Anybody else would've probably fired him."

"The other hands probably wish I would. When he doesn't show, it makes their load tougher. Everyone else has given up on him—his wife, his folks. But I know he's better than this. I keep hoping my support will somehow see him through." His gaze landed on her. "Why'd you pick tonight to hit your first bar?"

She rolled her eyes. "A couple of old high school friends are in town for a wedding. I thought we were going to the steakhouse down the street, but they piled out of my car and came here."

"I saw you come in a while after Geena Woods and Marcy Smithson."

She nodded. "I was afraid to sit in the car by myself. I think I got tricked into being their designated driver for the night."

"You never did fit in with them." Quinn's gaze cut to the PDA in the booth across the bar. He winced.

A slow song urged more couples to the dance floor. Cowboy boots scuffed and shuffled. A few of the dancers could barely stand, much less keep their rhythm.

"They were always wilder than me, tried to get me to go to parties. I thought surely they'd settled down and it was safe to go to dinner with them. Not." She sighed. "My whole family always ribs me about being gullible." She bit her lip. "If you see any of them, could you not mention this?"

"I don't go home much these days." He sipped his drink. "How is Star?"

"Married a jerk. She's divorced and lives in Denton now." *Moved there to be closer to me and wants me to move in with her. Like everybody else.* "So where is your ranch?"

"In a little town called Aubrey."

"You're kidding. I live in Aubrey."

The music sped to a faster beat, and the less-lit couples formed into a synchronized line dance.

"Small world. What have you been up to for the last ten years?" He scanned her left hand. "I know you got married. Any kids?"

Something sharp jabbed her heart, like it always did when people asked. She twisted her wedding rings. "I'm a widow."

"I'm sorry." His features pinched, as if he felt her pain. His hand moved toward hers but stopped a few inches away.

"Yeah. Me, too. But I have a little boy." That part always warmed her heart. Her life's joy. "How about you?"

"No kids. Never married. I guess I've been working too hard to take the time."

"What keeps you so busy?"

He cleared his throat. "Raising quarter horses. What do you say we get out of this place and get that bite to eat?"

"I can't leave them here—much as I'd like to. They deserve it, but I can't."

"Just to the steakhouse on the next block. You can tell them where we're going, and then I'll escort you safely back."

She glanced around the bar and located her two friends. Since Geena and Marcy were still *occupied*, why not? "Sounds great."

"From the looks of things back there, I don't think your friends will miss you." Quinn pulled a chair for her in the restaurant.

Lacie visibly relaxed, obviously more comfortable with her surroundings, as he claimed the seat across from her. She propped her elbow on the table, chin in her hand, and concentrated on the menu.

Country music twanged. Loud conversation and the clink of silverware surrounded them. He'd like to take her some-

where quiet, someplace with a dance floor. What he wouldn't give to Texas Two Step with Lacie Maxwell.

"What can I get you to drink?" The waitress shot him a flirty smile and never even looked at Lacie.

Lacie didn't seem to notice. "Unsweet tea, please."

"That's downright un-Texan. I'll take sweet."

Jaw-dropping gorgeous packed in a tiny stick of dynamite. He'd always admired her pint-sized beauty from afar. Miss popularity—from homecoming queen to rodeo queen. Practically engaged to someone else when they met, she'd barely known he existed. He'd wished many a time he'd met her first.

Time had only added to her beauty. Her blond hair was straighter, softer, not as big as it used to be. But she still loved rhinestones. They lined her jacket and jean pockets, adding to her natural sparkle.

Her menu lowered.

Caught red-handed staring at her. Busted. "How'd you end up in Aubrey?"

A sigh bigger than her huffed out. "Mel was from Wichita, Kansas, and always wanted to live in the country, so we found something 'small town' in the middle."

Mel? The name twisted in his gut.

"Now I'm at a crossroads. My landlord sold my house. I have to be out by the end of next month."

But he'd just found her again. "You going home?"

"I don't know." Her menu rose and he couldn't see her anymore. "My parents think my little boy needs to be closer to family, and Star wants me to move in with her. My friend owns a dude ranch in Aubrey and wants me to move into the suite at his ranch house."

Was the friend trying to worm his way into her heart? Or had he already? How long since her husband's death?

"I'll admit Aubrey hasn't been the same since—" Raw pain cut off her words.

Gently, Quinn pushed her menu down until he could see her face. "What do you want?"

Her eyes got shinier. "Nobody's asked me that in a while. I want…my life to be the way it used to be." She blinked several times. "But it's not going to happen, so I want to do what's best for my son. Trouble is, I'm not sure what that is. I've been praying about it."

The waitress brought the teas and waited to take their orders. He made a point not to look at her—courteous, but not interested in anyone other than Lacie.

Lacie added two yellow packets and downed nearly her whole glass. "I didn't realize how thirsty I am."

"I can see that." He grinned. "Why didn't you drink the Coke I got you at the bar?"

Pink tinged her cheeks. "I wasn't sure what else was in it, and I don't drink. Period."

"Me neither. I can assure you, it was just Coke."

"Oh well, Coke isn't as thirst-quenching anyway. It burns all the way down."

"True. But bars don't generally have tea." He took a long drink, letting the sweet coldness bathe his dry throat.

His gaze settled on Lacie, and he fell under the spell she'd cast on him almost ten years ago.

After all these years, he'd caught up with her again. But she'd probably be moving soon. Unless…was her friend the new man in her picture? Her reason for staying in Aubrey? Or maybe a career? He liked that thought better. "Do you work?"

Her pretty blue eyes squeezed shut. "No, Mel left me in pretty good shape with life insurance. And we had a nest egg."

Something twisted in his belly. "You shouldn't tell just anybody that. There are losers all over the place looking for widows with funds to take advantage of."

"But you're not just anybody. You're Quinn Remington. Good ol' boy from San Antone."

Bile coated the back of his throat as a familiar wave

washed over him. He used to be. Until he'd killed a man. He swallowed hard, pushing the guilt down, and forced a smile. "Did you work before your son was born?"

"I taught kids how to ride horses at my friend's ranch."

"I bet you were great."

"It was fun." Her eyes sparkled. "How did you get into raising quarter horses? Didn't you want to raise rodeo stock and such?"

His heart withered inside him. That dream took a wreck of a u-turn. "I decided on something tamer."

"If you just came to Aubrey and you haven't been home in a while, what about in-between?"

If only he could redo the in-between. "I had a ranch in the Southlake area."

"Wow, that's an expensive area. You've done well for yourself."

He couldn't get into his past. Had to steer her away. "Do you still barrel race?"

"Not for about five years."

"But you were so good, and you loved it. The prettiest rodeo queen of 'em all."

Her face reddened. "Mel's career required a lot of travel. For the last few years, I supported him—didn't have time for barrels. And since my son came, I have even less time."

"What kind of career did your husband have?"

Her throat convulsed. "Rodeo. At the pro level."

Wished he hadn't asked. "If you decide to stay in Aubrey, I could use a horse trainer at my ranch. I've got a guy who teaches adults to ride, but he's kind of gruff with kids. You could teach our future barrel racers."

Her eyes lit up. "I don't know. I'd love to get back into teaching kids. But I don't want to take time away from my son."

"Maybe part time?"

"Maybe."

"How old is your son?"

"He turned two in April." She sparkled. The boy was obviously her reason to live. "He's with my friends tonight." She checked her watch. "Hopefully in bed by now."

"How long since your husband… ? Never mind. Shouldn't have asked."

"Almost two and half years." Her voice, barely a whisper.

If her boy turned two four months ago, she'd been pregnant when her husband died. Bore their son alone. Raising him alone. "I'm really sorry. Must've been a hard row to hoe."

"I got Max to remember him by." She smiled. Genuine. "And he's so much like his daddy. We gave him my maiden name, Maxwell. I used to call him Little Mel, but a sensible friend sat me down and said, 'Now Lacie'"—she deepened her voice—"'He won't always be little. I know it's your way of honoring Mel, naming his boy after him, but the boy needs his own name.' So Little Mel became Max."

Her sensible friend was a man. The friend who wanted her to move into his ranch house? How good of a friend?

The server brought their food on a huge tray. Her steak was almost as big as his. Where would she put it?

Quinn unrolled his silverware from the cloth napkin.

"Ahem."

He met her gaze.

"Aren't you going to pray?"

He swallowed hard. Hadn't done that in a few years. "You go ahead."

"Thank You, Lord, for this food. For all the blessings You heap on us."

Blessings? Lacie's husband died, leaving her to raise her son alone. Where was the blessing in that?

"Help Geena and Marcy to realize they're not really living and to make better decisions in the future. Help them see something in me that leads them to You. Be with Quinn's

ranch hand, too. Give him strength to stop drinking. In Jesus' name, amen."

A dull ache hollowed out in his chest. He used to pray like that. Quinn cut his steak in silence, while she tore into hers. Big appetite for such a little thing.

"I think you helped me decide to stay in Aubrey."

"Really?" His insides warmed.

"I'm twenty-seven years old. Too old to go running home to Mama and Daddy. I'm not a city girl anymore, so that rules out San Antonio and Denton." She blew out a big breath. "I've felt so much pressure from all sides, I couldn't think clearly. Sometimes just saying it all out loud clarifies things. Thanks."

"Glad to be of help." She'd be sticking around. But moving into her friend's ranch suite. What kind of friend? "Reckon you'll be packing up soon then."

"Yeah. I'm glad Mel and I didn't get around to building a house, since I don't have to worry about paying for it. God works things out for the best."

Not always. "I wish things had turned out better for you, but I'm glad you're planning to stay for the time being, Lacie Maxwell. Let me know if you're interested in that job."

"Gentry."

Quinn's fork clattered to the table. "What?"

"It's Gentry. Lacie Gentry."

Her words shot through his heart. No. No. No. Mel Gentry. It couldn't be.

Chapter 2

Quinn paled before her eyes.

Lacie touched his hand. "Are you okay?"

"Fine. I'm not as hungry as I thought." He set his knife down.

"Well, I am. You're gonna make me look like a hog." She eyed his barely touched steak.

"Want mine, too?"

"Don't tempt me." She grinned.

She'd always liked Quinn. He'd moved to San Antonio during their senior year. At school and church, he'd been nice and gentlemanly. She might've worked harder at getting to know him, if she hadn't already met Mel at a rodeo and been focused on their long-distance relationship.

"Do you need help moving?" Quinn plowed fork tracks through his baked potato. "I've got lots of stock trailers, perfect for moving."

"I don't have much furniture and no appliances to move. A pickup would do it, but you'd really do that?"

"Sure. Why not?"

"I planned to hire one of those moving companies."

"Do you have any idea how much that costs?"

She closed her eyes. "Unfortunately. But remember, I'm pretty well set. Not rich—by any means—but I can handle it."

"No need to spend it when you don't have to."

Tempting, but she couldn't take advantage of his generosity. "Still. It's too much to ask."

"You didn't ask. I offered."

"I'll think about it." She put her fork down and pushed her plate away. "I can't hold another bite. And I'm afraid I'd better get back to the bar and force some people to leave." It was getting late. Rayna would pepper her with questions when she returned.

He caught the server's attention, motioned for the bill, and pulled out his wallet.

"I'll get dinner." Lacie picked up her purse.

"You most certainly won't. I've never let a woman pay for my meal, and I won't start now."

"If not for me, you'd have seen your employee wasn't at the bar and gone home."

"But I'm glad I was there to rescue you."

The server brought the bill, and Quinn put the money in the leather folder.

"At least let me pay for my part."

"It's taken care of. Ready?" He offered his arm.

She accepted, knowing she'd want his protection once they got back to the bar. "I'll buy next time, then."

"Next time?" He winked. "I like the sound of that."

Her heart squeezed. She hadn't meant to lead him on. There wouldn't be a next time. She hadn't been this close to a man in two and half years, except her dad or Clay, who was like a brother to her. She didn't plan to make a habit of it.

She loosened her grip on his arm and put some space between them. "I mean—if I let you help me move."

"You mean—*when*, since I don't plan on taking no for an answer."

Quinn's eyes adjusted to the dim lighting. An all-too-familiar drunk sat at the bar. Quinn blew out a big breath.

"What's wrong?" Lacie huddled closer to him.

He liked the feeling of having her near and serving as her protector. He owed her so much more. "That employee I didn't find earlier—Hank's the one slumped over on the bar."

"A shame." She looked Hank over. "He's just a kid. So young to already have a drinking problem."

"Yeah, he's barely legal, but he started a long time ago. Out of his own daddy's personal stash."

"Sad." She scanned the bar, dance floor, and tables. "I don't see Geena or Marcy."

"I'll ask the bartender." Quinn's blood boiled. They'd duped Lacie into going to a bar for the first time in her life. Yet she'd stayed to make sure they got home okay—and they had the nerve to disappear on her.

Quinn stepped up to the bar. "Excuse me. Did you happen to notice the blond and the brunette who were with my friend here?"

"They left with a couple of bozos. Said to give her this note." He handed the note to Lacie.

"Thanks." She unfolded it and pressed trembling fingertips to her lips. "I can't believe they left with men they don't even know."

"There aren't many women like you, Lacie."

"I wish there were. I mean—I'm not perfect by any means—but moral at least."

Perfect in his estimation. From the top of her blond head to the pointy toes of her sequin-splashed cowgirl boots. He steered her toward the door.

"But what about your friend?"

Hank hadn't stirred at all. "I don't think he's going any-where. I'll see you safely to your car, and then I'll get him out of here."

Quinn pressed his hand to the small of her back. He'd wanted to touch Lacie Maxwell for almost ten years. Now that he could, he had no right. His hand fell to his side.

His mission in Aubrey would be easier since he'd already met Mel Gentry's widow. By accident, he'd already put his plan into practice. Tonight he'd become her rescuing knight. He only wished Mel Gentry's widow weren't Lacie.

She pressed her clicker to unlock her metallic-gold SUV. He opened the door for her. "Make sure it starts up."

She scooted in, turned the key, and the engine roared to life. "Thanks for everything."

"Let me know when you get ready to move." The very least he could do, since he'd ruined her life.

He shut the door and watched as she merged onto the highway. Her lights faded from view, and he headed back to the bar.

Lacie smoothed downy blond hair from Max's temple. Sleeping soundly, angelic expression, breathing so sweetly and gently. Tears came to her eyes. Her baby boy was grow-ing up so fast.

Clay had pulled out the hide-a-bed in the nursery and stacked a wall of pillows around Max.

Cool air blew from the vent. She adjusted the thin blan-ket tighter around his shoulders, dropped a kiss on his soft cheek, and tiptoed from the nursery.

Rodeo pictures, mostly of Clay, a few of his dad and Mel, lined the cedar walls in the hallway.

She stopped in front of one of his photos. His last season, one of his final rodeos. The familiar face she loved, framed

by dark hair. His deep brown eyes looked into her soul. Had he known what she'd done?

Her fingertips traced the crevices in his strong jaw, but the glass was cold. She jerked her hand away and pressed it to her trembling lips.

Was there stress in the lines around his eyes? Stress she'd put there? Had he wanted it to be his last season? Or had she forced his decision?

If only she could have a do-over. Hold off having a baby until Mel retired, but it was too late. Had she had a part in his death?

No. Only God controlled life and death. But she may have made his last days less happy. She'd hold herself accountable for that until the day she joined him in heaven.

She scurried down the hall to the guestroom. Clay had told her to spend the night if Max was asleep when she got back. It made sense, but she wanted to go home. To the bed she'd shared with Mel. The bed that wouldn't be hers for much longer.

"You're in awfully late."

Lacie skidded to a halt with a little yelp. Busted by Rayna. Like a teenager. Only, being late hadn't been her fault, other than being stupid.

"Clay said you're staying here for the night. Our extra room's at your service."

"I hadn't planned to, but I hate to wake Max."

"Let him sleep. Did you have a nice time?"

"It was a nice dinner." Pulled it off without a hitch in her tone and continued to the guestroom.

The room blended Rayna's contemporary tastes with Clay's down-home country flair—a handmade red, black, and gray quilt in fashionable fabrics covered the bed, matching curtains and area rug paired with raw-pine furnishings and walls. A mix of both their personalities, completely in sync and honest with each other—the way a marriage should be.

"I'm sorry you had to get Max down. I meant to be back sooner."

Rayna perched on the foot of the guest bed. "No problem. I rocked Kayla to sleep, and then Clay took a shift in the rocker with Max. They both went out like a light."

"How's Kayla's teething?"

"Settling down." Rayna patted her arm. "I'm glad you had a good time. You need to get out more. Did you meet any men?"

Lacie worked at keeping her expression composed. "Why?"

"I thought I caught a whiff of men's cologne."

Something tingled in her stomach. Rayna should've been a detective. "I ran into a guy I graduated with. He escorted me to my car."

"Awesome. Is he a good catch?"

Her heart clenched. "I'm not fishing."

Rayna patted her arm again. "Oh sweetie, I know you miss Mel. I do, too. But you're young. He wouldn't want you to be alone."

Her breath stalled. She stood and turned her back on Rayna. "Please. I'm not ready."

"It's been over two years."

Two years, five months—she checked her watch—*three hours, and forty-three minutes*. "I'm not ready. And I have to focus on Max."

"Who could use a good daddy."

"He has a daddy."

"I know, and you do a great job keeping Mel alive for him, but he needs a living, breathing daddy."

Lacie shook her head. "No man could love him like his own daddy. I'm the only one who can love him through and through like he deserves."

"But Lacie—"

She raised her hand and faced her friend. "Stop. I made a decision. I'm moving to the ranch until I decide what to do."

"Wonderful." Rayna clasped her hands together as if a prayer had been answered.

"But I won't if I have to deal with this conversation on a daily basis. The subject is closed."

"Understood." Rayna's mouth clamped tight.

"I know you love me and you're trying to help, but—"

"What are you gals up to?" Clay leaned against the doorframe. "Past bedtime for all mommies."

"Lacie's moving in your old suite over at the ranch house."

Clay looked as if he might jump up and down. "We can repaint. Whatever will make you comfortable."

"I really appreciate y'all. You've been great since Mel's accident, really great. But I'm a grown woman; this isn't permanent."

Rayna's mouth twitched. "But permanent will be somewhere close, I hope?"

"But no pressure." Clay shot her a lopsided grin. "Start packing up tomorrow, and we'll get you situated."

"I don't want you hurting your shoulder. I might know someone who can help."

"My shoulder's good as new." Clay rotated it for proof.

"The guy from high school?" Rayna tried for nonchalance but couldn't pull it off.

"What guy?" Clay drawled.

Lacie sighed. "Maybe I should hire a mover after all."

"Lacie ran into an old friend tonight. But not another word about it." Rayna pressed a finger to her lips.

"As usual when females are around, I think I missed something." Clay winked at his wife. "Night, Lace."

Lacie blew out a sigh, her eyes fixed on Quinn's business card. A warm breeze fluttered the pages of her magazine as she sat on the back deck of her and Mel's rental house. But Mel didn't live here anymore. And hadn't in a long time.

Max played in the sandbox, digging with his neon-green

plastic shovel. Even though Clay insisted on setting up a tent canopy over Max's play area, she'd slathered her son in co-conut-scented sun block. He was now coated in grit, despite her caution to let it dry first, and happy that way.

None of the movers in the Dallas-Fort Worth area or Denton could get her moved until next month. She had to be out before then. No sense prolonging it. It would be hard enough to leave this house.

Leaving behind the life she'd built with Mel.

Get it over with. Fast. She closed her eyes.

"Mama, look." Max held up a granddaddy longlegs by one hair-like limb.

"Yes baby. But remember, don't pick up just any spider. Only granddaddies won't hurt you. And be careful. Don't hurt him."

He gently set the spider down and continued building a sandcastle.

Make the phone calls and she could go play in the sand with her son. But she didn't want to call her parents. Or Quinn. Especially after what Rayna had said. Would he think she was interested in him?

Surely Clay could round up some ranch hands to help. But she knew how hard they worked. She couldn't ask them to help her move after a hard day's work.

Procrastination. She set the phone book down and punched in her parents' number—the lesser of the two dreads.

"Hello?" Mama's voice tugged at her. Homesick. Not for San Antonio, just for her parents.

"Hey Mama, I've decided to move into Clay's ranch house for now."

A gasp. "Your father and I were hoping you'd come home."

"I know, Mama. And I thought about it, but it's just not home to me anymore." Her fingers tightened on the arm of the lawn chair.

"We miss you and Max so."

"I know. But we come visit a lot, and y'all come here, too. Every two months or so, we're together."

"Do you need help moving?"

Acceptance. "No. I was going to hire movers, but Rayna and Clay offered to help. And so did Quinn Remington. The house was furnished and so is the ranch suite, so I don't have appliances or furniture to move, except for Max's."

"Quinn Remington? The Quinn Remington I know?"

How did she let that slip? Her gaze rose to the sky. Two smoky jet trails intersected perfectly at a crossroads in the almost-cloudless blue. Like her horizon.

"I ran into him the other day." At a bar. Laughter bubbled up her throat. "He lives in Aubrey now."

"Really? I always liked that boy. And you know he had a crush on you in high school."

"No." Lacie shook her head, as if her mother could see her. "We were only friends."

"Maybe on your part, but he always stared at you when you weren't looking. And he never married. Maybe because he never got over you."

"You're reading way too much into this, Mama. And besides, like I told Rayna, I'm not ready." Her wedding rings glistened in the sun.

"I know, sweetheart. But someday your heart will open again. Maybe God's been saving Quinn to open it. He's a Christian, and he'd make a right fine daddy for Max."

Tell her about the bar. That would call her off. Maybe, but then Mama would redouble her efforts to convince Lacie to move home. Oh, why did Mel have to die? Why did everything have to be so hard?

"Can you please not marry me off just yet?" Raw pain echoed in her words—the pain of letting Mel down, of missing him and making decisions on her own, of raising their son without him.

But she wasn't alone. Jesus was with her. Sometimes she

had to remind herself to lean on Him more. And consult Him with decisions.

"Let us know when you get settled. Your daddy and I will come for a visit."

"Sounds nice. Bye, Mama."

The phone rang in her hand.

She jumped with a little yelp. "Hello?"

"Lacie, it's Quinn. I found your number in the book and called to see when I can help you move."

Quinn knocked on the door.

Footfalls sounded, and it swung open. Lacie, as pretty as ever. Her typical rhinestone-studded denim with a simple white T-shirt. Turquoise jewelry made her eyes look the same shade.

"You're right on time. My friend already took one load to his ranch, but he should be back anytime."

So her friend was a man, and she was moving there. Pressure built in his chest. A multitude of stacked cardboard boxes sat in the middle of the room. "Any particular starting place?"

"Grab a box, I reckon."

Quinn scooped up one to load.

"No—" The word ripped from Lacie's throat. Hands shaking, she reached for the box. Her too-shiny eyes met his. "I'll take this one."

Chapter 3

Quinn read the words scrawled in black marker across the cardboard. Fragile. Wedding Pictures.

Fragile—like Lacie.

"It's heavy." Quinn managed to keep his tone steady. "I'll be real careful. You want it in your car?"

She bit her lip and let him take the box. "In the front."

Trust shone in her eyes. If only she knew.

He carried Lacie's *heart* out to her SUV.

She hurried ahead of him and opened the door.

Gently, he wedged the box in the floorboard, making sure it wouldn't topple if she hit the break.

"Thank you." She turned back to the house.

He followed.

Why had this friend offered her a place to live? Was he worthy of Lacie? Or some jerk trying to take advantage of her grief—and bank account? But if he owned a ranch house, he must be relatively solvent. Unless he was in over his head.

Quinn leaned against the doorjamb. "Where's Max today?"

"Rayna took him home with her."

Rayna? He wanted to ask who that was, but the intricacies of her life and relationships were none of his business. He picked up a box marked Dishes. "You want all the glass in your car?"

"Yes please." She scooted a box across the floor with her foot. "How's Hank?"

"Working, for the time being. Had one dilly of a hangover the other day."

Lacie looked out the living room window. "Here he is."

The bare windows gave a clear view of a dark-green Dodge 4x4 Crew Cab pulling into Lacie's drive. Not brand new, but late model. Did this guy have money—or need Lacie's to pay for his toys? A man jumped down from the truck then helped a pretty redhead climb down. He looked familiar.

Without knocking, the woman entered first. "Hey Lacie, I got Max down for his nap, and Clay's mama is supervising, so I came back to help."

"Great." Lacie hugged her. "I don't know what I'd do without y'all."

"You're Clay Warren." The words popped out of Quinn's mouth.

"I am, and this is my wife, Rayna."

The pressure seeped out of his lungs. Lacie's friend was married and harmless—besides being a four-time CBR Bull Riding Champ, though recently retired. Quinn didn't know Clay, but his rep was that of a stand-up kind of guy.

"This is Quinn Remington, an old high school friend." Lacie labeled another box with her marker. "He offered to help me move."

The pungent odor of permanent ink burned his nostrils.

"I know that name," Clay said. "You bought the place a few ranches over from ours."

"So that makes you our neighbor." Rayna's gaze cut to Lacie then back to him. A satisfied smile settled in place.

"Small world, indeed. Hey, I'm cooking at our house tonight and inviting a few friends over to welcome Lacie. Clay's mom is keeping all the kids, so it'll be relaxing. You should join us."

"She makes a mean chicken enchilada." Clay winked at his wife.

"Who am I to turn down a home-cooked meal?" Or time spent with Lacie.

"Great." Rayna scooped up a box.

They loaded Quinn's pickup, and he helped Clay with the toddler bed and chest of drawers from the nursery.

"This is the easiest move I've ever helped with." Clay clapped him on the back. "That's all the furniture."

"Watch that shoulder, tough guy." Rayna met them. "This is the last of the glass. Everything else can go in the truck beds."

Back in the house, Quinn grabbed a box. "What's with your shoulder? Should you be lifting that?"

"Rotator cuff surgery. It's been almost two years, but Rayna still worries." Clay headed out with a load.

Must be nice to have a woman to worry.

Lacie stood at the end of the hall, staring into what looked like the master bedroom. She dug in her pocket and raised a tissue to her face.

His heart hurt even worse than usual. Quinn hurried to his truck. "I imagine leaving the house where she lived with him is tough on her."

Clay shifted boxes around in his pickup bed for a better fit. "Like she's turning her back on him."

"She doesn't have much choice." Quinn wiped sweat from his forehead. "The house sold."

"I know. But she doesn't see it that way."

"You've known her a long time?"

"Mel was the best friend I ever had. She's like the sister I never had, so I watch out for her."

"I'm glad."

Clay kicked at a pebble with the toe of his boot. "I don't think she's ready to start anything new. Don't push her."

"I'm just here to help out." Quinn splayed his hands in surrender.

"Just saying. In case you get any ideas. She's a right pretty little thing—inside and out." Clay's gaze bored a hole through him. "Just know that if you hurt her, you deal with me."

What would Clay do if he learned the truth? That Quinn had already hurt her? Before he'd ever reconnected with her. With a mortal wound straight to her heart. But he wouldn't hurt her anymore. He'd be there, help her, protect her. But that's all. No matter what his heart wanted.

"Got it. I know she's alone and vulnerable. I'd like to help out where I can. And to tell you the truth, I worried about you. She called you her friend, but I'd pegged you as some guy out to take advantage of her."

Clay laughed. "Glad we understand each other."

"Better get busy." Quinn hurried to the house.

Sniffling greeted him. Rayna hugged a crying Lacie in the empty walk-in closet. "It's silly. I mean, what am I gonna do with his clothes—but I can't get rid of them, not yet."

No, Lacie definitely wasn't ready for anything new. He'd just have to keep reminding his heart of that fact. Besides, if she knew the truth, she'd run the other way as fast as she could. And he didn't have the right to pick up her pieces when he was the one who broke her life.

Lacie scanned the stripped-of-personal-items house. Only the rental furnishings remained. Another piece of Mel she'd leave behind. They'd been happy here. But it hadn't been the same since he died. Maybe new surroundings would be a good thing. She rubbed her palms up and down her arms.

"Ahem."

She turned. Sweat soaked the hair around Quinn's heat-reddened face. "Sorry for picking such a hot month to move."

"Not your fault. Sorry to interrupt, but do you want me to take down the curtains in the kitchen? I noticed all the others are gone."

"Those hideous roosters." She held up both hands toward the curtains, as if to block the view. "One of the meanest critters on God's green earth. They can stay."

He grinned. "Why did you buy them if you don't like roosters?"

"Mel thought they were manly. Obviously, he never faced a real one on the attack."

"Everything's loaded then. Take your time."

The door clicked closed.

I won't cry. I won't cry. I won't cry.

Especially since she'd already cried twice today.

Head held high, she forced one foot in front of the other. Deep breaths. Face the future.

Without Mel.

Traverse the obstacle course of life—Quinn thrown into her dinner plans by a well-meaning Rayna. Maybe she'd stay in her suite tonight. But that would be rude, and Quinn had helped her move.

At the door now. Turn the knob, that's right. Now, walk out. Don't look back, only forward.

Quinn sat in his truck in front of Clay and Rayna's house. He shouldn't have come. No matter how badly he wanted to be near Lacie, nothing could come of it. Only torture—for no reason—and he didn't need any more torture. Nor did she.

A truck pulled in behind him, its headlights spotlighting him. He got out, his overheated skin immediately missing the air-conditioned cab.

A door opened and closed. A couple holding hands strolled toward him.

"Adam Landers and my wife, Gabby." Adam offered his free hand. "I'm Rayna's brother."

"Quinn Remington."

"Rayna said you graduated with Lacie." Gabby, pregnant, brunette, and bubbly, did a little bounce on the balls of her feet.

News traveled fast in this circle of friends.

"Let's get this party started." Adam headed for the house.

Quinn followed, his stomach in a knot. Should've left while he had the chance.

The house bustled with activity and greetings. Country charm with lots of wood accents and modern furnishings.

"Hey, you made it." Rayna patted his arm. "Dinner's almost ready. Find a seat."

Lacie sat on the red leather couch. Alone.

He wanted to join her but claimed a matching chair across the room instead.

Another knock and a familiar woman entered, followed by a cowboy. The woman's hair was long, straight, and soft brown. Blue eyes. Where did he know her from?

Her gaze met his. Her smile froze.

And it all came back to him.

Lacie was used to being odd gal out with her married friends, but Quinn made it even. And she didn't need an even.

"This is Kendra and Stetson, our friends." Rayna introduced the latest arrivals to Quinn. "Kendra is the photographer at the ad agency where I work, and Stetson is a rodeo clown—I mean, bullfighter—at the Stockyards, and the youth director at our church."

The two men shook hands.

Stetson scratched his stubbly chin. "Didn't you used to announce at the rodeo over at Mesquite?"

Quinn's throat convulsed. "A few years back."

"I worked there, too. Guess you didn't recognize me without my grease paint."

"The only man I know who wears makeup to work." Rayna

elbowed Stetson. "Y'all make yourself at home. I'll have dinner ready in a minute. Speaking of which, I'd better go see about it."

"I'll help." Lacie jumped to her feet.

"Me, too." Kendra seemed nervous.

"You're not leaving me stuck with the menfolk." Gabby heaved her eight-month belly forward and awkwardly stood.

Rayna tsk-tsked. "Gabby, those ankles look like they need to be propped up."

"Thanks for pointing out the balloons I used to call ankles. I'll prop 'em on a chair in the kitchen."

"Still beautiful ankles." Adam slapped Gabby's derrière.

Lacie's heart squeezed. Some of her last moments with Mel were sweet like that, her feeling like a whale, and him trying to convince her she was beautiful.

The women trailed to the kitchen. The TV clicked on. The clap of a ball in the glove and the crack of the bat followed by shouts from the crowd.

"Get the feeling they were waiting for us to leave?" Rayna opened the oven door then shut it. "Looks like another ten minutes should do it."

Usually talkative, Kendra stared out the window. Though she'd originally been Rayna's friend, she and Lacie had shared several rodeos since Clay's retirement and grown close.

"Kendra, you okay?" Lacie touched her elbow. "You seem kind of distracted."

"I'm fine. I hate leaving Danielle with a sitter."

"Clay's mama can handle all three kids, hands tied behind her back, I promise." Lacie grabbed a stack of plates from the cupboard.

"It's not that. I'm terrified Lynn will change her mind and want Danielle back. I don't want to miss any time with her, just in case."

"You know Danielle's biological mother?" Lacie frowned.

"Too well." Kendra hugged herself. "Lynn was in our youth group before Stetson and I married."

"Has she said anything about changing her mind?" Lacie circled the table, setting places as she went.

"No."

"She gave her up for adoption." Rayna clinked ice in the glasses. "You and Stetson signed the papers."

"But she's the biological mother."

Lacie took Kendra's hand and squeezed it. "I'll tell you what my mama always said: 'Don't go borrowing trouble.'"

"That's what Stetson says. I shouldn't have come. My funk will ruin everyone's evening." Kendra rushed to the door. "I'm gonna go out to the barn and try to pull it together."

"Want my funk to keep yours company?" Lacie grinned.

"Thanks, but I only need a minute."

Lacie exchanged a worried glance with Rayna.

Movement out the window caught Quinn's attention. Kendra. Hands shoved in her jean's pockets, she strolled out to the barn. She was prettier now. The harsh black hair and fuchsia highlights were gone.

All the other men were intent on the baseball game. He stood and slipped out, forcing himself to take his time getting to the barn. An eternity.

She sat on a hay bale, holding an orange kitten. Her mouth opened then closed. "What are you doing here?"

"Lacie and I went to high school together. I helped her move this afternoon, and Rayna invited me tonight."

She shook her head. "I mean, following me to the barn."

Sweat tickled a trail down his back. "I felt like getting out of that wonderfully air-conditioned house and coming out here in this oppressive heat where it's hard to even breathe." He inhaled deep lungsful of manure-scented air.

His attempt at humor didn't draw even a glimmer of a smile out of her. In a bind—and he was definitely in one—

the truth usually worked. "I figured you're as uncomfortable as me. I thought if we talked it out, it might help."

"I'm not the same person I was that night." Her posture straightened. "I'm a Christian now."

"I'm glad. Sad thing is—I was a Christian then." He pulled a straw from a hay bale and clamped it between his teeth. Sweet and stale at the same time.

"Stetson had a hard time with my past when we first met." She blew out a sigh. "We're happily married, and we adopted a little girl. We've built a good life together."

And she thought he'd jeopardize what they'd built. Why shouldn't she, after the impression he'd given her in that bar? It was all she knew of him.

His shoulders slumped. "I have no intention of messing it up for you."

A trembly sigh escaped. "Thank you. Lacie's been through a lot. She doesn't need anyone messing with her either."

"Believe it or not, Kendra, the man you met in that bar two and a half years ago wasn't me. Yes, I was backslidden"—and still on the outs with God—"but I was never the drunken, one-night-stand type. I haven't had a drop since. Or another night like that."

"Wish I could say the same thing." She shrugged. "But it took me a little longer to turn my life around."

"I don't want to be uncomfortable around you if we meet up again." He sighed. "I'd like a second chance to make a first impression on you. Let's put that night to rest. Like it never happened."

Her gaze narrowed. "Nothing happened anyway."

"Only because I was too drunk to take something from you I had no right to."

Kendra winced. "If I remember right, I offered."

"Nevertheless, I'm sorry."

In the distance, a cow bawled, piercing the silence between them.

"Me, too—you were in rough shape that night, and I should've left you alone."

"I was reeling from…life. I turned to the bottle instead of Jesus." How long had it been since he'd even said that name? Odd how naturally it popped out of his mouth, like they were still on speaking terms.

"I know exactly what you were reeling from. You told me all about it."

Quinn's heart sped to triple time.

"Does Lacie know?" Kendra asked.

Chapter 4

Quinn cleared his throat. "I hadn't seen her since graduation until I ran into her in Fort Worth. I didn't know who her husband was."

"So what are you up to with her?" Kendra picked up a kitten and cuddled it.

"Nothing. I reckon I feel like I owe her. I want to help out."

"You have to tell her who you are."

He nodded and gripped the metal gate of a horse stall. Lacie would hate him if she knew the truth—and he wasn't sure he could handle that.

"If things were to develop between you, and then she found out, it would all blow."

"Trust me, nothing's going to develop." He didn't deserve her.

"Listen, what happened that night wasn't your fault. But she needs to know."

"Needs to know what?" the male voice said behind Quinn.

Kendra's eyes widened.

Quinn winced, spun around.

Yep. Her husband. Looking ready to kill.

Kendra cleared her throat. "Could Stetson and I have some privacy, please?"

She shouldn't have to face her husband's potential wrath on her own, since Quinn was just as guilty for what could've happened between them. Maybe she wouldn't tell him, but it was her call. Not his.

"Listen, Stetson, this isn't what it looks like. Your wife loves you, and in my book—married women are off limits."

Stetson's jaw clenched.

Quinn risked one more glance at Kendra then left the barn. Any minute, Stetson might waylay him from behind. And he'd deserve it. He didn't look back.

His truck beckoned in the drive. But Rayna had been kind enough to invite him tonight. He had to go back to the house. At least for a little while.

Lacie stepped off the back porch and met Quinn halfway down the path. "What were you doing in the barn with Kendra?" She tried to keep the suspicion out of her expression and tone.

"I didn't know she was out there. Just needed some air."

"They're happily married." Lacie's hands propped on her hips. "And Kendra has a lot on her plate."

Quinn held up his hands in a hands-off gesture. "Marriage has my highest respect."

"Good." Her gaze narrowed, measuring him. But she couldn't read anything in his expression. "Food's ready. I was coming to get Kendra."

"Great. I'm starved." He glanced at his truck, eagerness to escape written all over his tense posture.

Good, maybe he'd leave. She whirled toward the house.

He fell in step beside her.

Frayed nerves stretched to a breaking point. She hurried

her pace. But then, he might be checking out her backside. She slowed and ended up beside him again.

Inside the house, Rayna and Gabby bustled around the table.

But what was going on in the barn? Kendra had gone out. Then as Lacie started out to get her for the meal, she saw Stetson go in. Hesitant to interrupt, she'd stalled on the porch. Moments later, Quinn exited.

Had he followed Kendra?

Quinn looked out the window, and Lacie followed his gaze. Stetson and Kendra headed for the driveway, their expressions taut.

Sucking in a deep breath, Quinn turned away.

An engine started up. Lacie's gaze met Quinn's. Still measuring. Still nothing.

Adam entered the kitchen, followed by Clay.

"Wonder why Stetson and Kendra left." Clay wound his arm around Rayna's waist.

"They left?" Rayna handed him a glass of tea. "I think Kendra had baby withdrawals."

True. But Lacie had the distinct impression that whatever happened in the barn was the reason they'd left.

And the reason Quinn avoided her eyes.

Lacie sank into the bed, emotionally and physically drained. First night at the ranch-house suite. At least Max had gone down easy in the next room.

The silver-framed picture of Mel sat on her nightstand. One of the last of his photos taken before she'd told him she was pregnant. No stress or worries in his features, only happiness, taken right before a rodeo. He'd always been happiest before a rodeo. Until she'd told him she was pregnant.

Her favorite paisley sheets were on the new bed. But she'd never slept with Mel in this bed. Thankfully, she'd never

washed his pillowcase. She buried her nose in it, savoring the faint scent of his spicy cologne. Faded, but still there.

Some psychiatrist would have a field day with her. She giggled. Mel's clothes were packed up in a box now, but she still had his pillow to smell. Tears stung, and her laughter ended on a sob. She pressed a hand against her mouth and snuggled deeper in the covers.

The king-size bed felt a mile wide. Empty and cold.

"Jesus," she whispered, "wrap Your arms around me. I'm so lonely."

Sweet peace and comfort enveloped her like a soft blanket. She closed her eyes.

The lie he'd told Lacie turned bitter in Quinn's gut. He'd definitely known Kendra was in the barn. Just hadn't expected to get busted. By her husband—no less.

He swiped sweat from his brow with his shoulder. Why did fences have to need repairs in August? Couldn't they wait until November to buckle and pull loose?

He couldn't tell Lacie he knew Kendra. Or what had almost happened between them. Or what had driven him to the bar.

How bad had the mess in the barn exploded after he left? Neither Kendra or Stetson looked happy when they left.

Gravel crunched in the driveway, and he straightened from repairing the slat in the rail fence. A blue Chevy 4x4. The door opened, and Stetson Wright vaulted out.

Ready to kill him.

He deserved it.

"Kendra told me what happened." Stetson's tone and posture stiffened. "I mean—what didn't happen."

"I'm sorry." Quinn leaned his hand on the fence. "You have to believe me. I'm a different man than I was then."

Stetson's mouth twitched. He nodded. "Kendra's past is done. Including your part in it." He shoved his hand toward Quinn.

Quinn braced himself for the blow. But it didn't come.

He glanced at Stetson's hand then clasped it. "The only reason I went to the barn last night was in case we keep running into each other. I didn't want her to feel uncomfortable around me."

"She told me. Said you were the perfect gentlemen. She also told me why you were at the bar the night y'all met."

Quinn's gaze dropped to the sun-baked grass.

"Did you know Clay Warren and Mel Gentry were best friends?"

Quinn nodded. "Warren dedicated his last season in Gentry's honor."

"What are you up to, Remington?" Stetson took off his hat. "Of all the ranches in Texas, why did you buy the one in Aubrey near Mel Gentry's best friend? And his widow?"

"I didn't know Lacie was his widow." He blew out a sigh. "I knew Gentry's widow lived somewhere near. But I didn't know she was the Lacie Maxwell I graduated with."

"But you purposely moved near them? Why?"

"I'm not sure." Quinn rubbed the back of his hand over his brow. "Penance. I thought maybe I could be neighborly. Help 'em out anyway I could. To make up for…"

Stetson adjusted his hat. "I've even questioned what would have happened if I'd been there that night, still working as a pickup man. But it's rodeo. It's part of the sport."

"I knew going in someone could get hurt or even die." Quinn's jaw clenched. "But when it happened, I felt responsible."

"No one in their right mind would blame you for Mel's death."

Guess that makes me not in my right mind.

"But why have you come now? When they're both beginning to heal."

Because I need to find healing. Quinn met his gaze.

"It will bring his death back when they learn who you are. You need to tell them. Or move on."

"What if I don't tell 'em and I keep hanging around? You gonna tell?"

"It's not my place. It's not Kendra's, either. It's yours." Stetson jabbed his finger at him and turned toward his truck.

Quinn's place, but how could he tell them? They'd blame him like he blamed himself. It was his fault. No matter what Stetson said, Quinn had killed Mel Gentry as sure as if he'd shot him at point-blank range.

Lacie sat between Rayna and Kendra. New church, without Mel.

Her heart sank to her stomach.

With the move, it made sense to change churches. Besides, even after more than two years, every time she went to their old church, she imagined Mel's casket in front of the pulpit. At least that memory wasn't tied to this church.

But too many changes were ganging up on her.

The navy-blue padded pews cushioned her back. Plenty of bookracks held a nice selection of hymnals and Bibles. The frosted windows kept out the sun's glare. Temperature, cool and comfortable. The people were nice and welcoming. How could she feel so lost?

Max shifted on her lap.

"You can take him to the nursery," Rayna whispered.

"We'll work up to it. Let him get to know people here first."

"It'll be my turn to work the nursery in a few weeks. It'll be a good time to transition him."

"He's usually pretty quiet. I kept him with me part of the time in our old church, so he'd learn how to sit and be quiet for the sermon."

"How are you feeling about everything?" Rayna patted her arm.

Everyone else on the pew was part of a couple. Clay and Rayna, Stetson and Kendra, Adam and Gabby. All the children were in the nursery. Lacie and Max were odd ones out, as usual.

"Lots of changes."

"You know we all love you and Max. We'll do whatever we can to help you adjust."

"I know." Her eyes stung, and she blinked. "Y'all have been great."

But her friends could only do so much. They couldn't take away her loneliness, her guilt, or the daunting task of raising her son. Alone.

She glanced at Kendra and Stetson. Not their usual talkative selves this morning. Something to do with Quinn?

What had happened in the barn the other night? She couldn't work for a man who caused problems for her friends. And why did her thoughts stray to him so often?

Lacie reined Copper into the long gravel drive. White rail fences lined each side. In the distance, Stetson drove his tractor.

Good, she and Kendra wouldn't be interrupted. She had to get to the bottom of the barn incident before she could decide on the carrot Quinn dangled in front of her. Oh, to work with horses and kids again, but not if Quinn had done anything to hurt her friend.

Soon as church ended yesterday, Kendra and Stetson left. And they hadn't shown up at Moms on Main, their typical eating place after morning services. Something was definitely going on.

Lacie neared the house and slowed the horse's gait. Dust swirled.

Kendra sat on the porch, rocking Danielle against her shoulder. She waved as Lacie dismounted.

"Is she asleep?" Lacie whispered, tying Copper to the porch rail.

"Yes, but nothing could wake her. Come join me." She rhythmically patted Danielle's back. "Did you ever think I'd be this content sitting on the porch of a farmhouse in Aubrey, Texas?"

"The right man can change lots of things." Lacie had dreamed of being a barrel racer. But Mel came along, and suddenly her dreams didn't matter. She claimed the wooden rocker beside Kendra.

"So what are you doing out our way?"

"Why did you leave Rayna's the other night? I'm worried about you."

"I hope we didn't hurt Rayna's feelings. She loves her get-togethers. And I do, too, but I wanted to be with Danielle."

"I know it's none of my business, but did Quinn upset you? I saw him coming from the barn before you and Stetson left."

"No." She took a deep breath. "Quinn and I met once. A long time ago. In a bar. Nothing happened, but he wanted to make sure I didn't feel uncomfortable around him."

Thank goodness. He hadn't made a pass at Kendra or tried to cause trouble between her and Stetson. But still... "He sure spends a lot of time in bars for someone who supposedly doesn't drink."

"Why do you say that?"

Lacie giggled. "Oh, I don't know. Maybe because I ran into him in a bar."

Kendra's eyes widened. "What were you doing there?"

"Relax. It was against my will." Lacie rolled her eyes. "Remember those friends of mine from high school who were in town for a wedding?"

Kendra nodded.

"They invited me out to dinner and then conveniently took me to a bar instead."

"You should have called us. We'd have come and gotten you."

"I get accused of being gullible a lot, so don't tell Rayna." Lacie's cheeks warmed. "I decided to handle it myself."

"I'll tell you what I tell our youth group—if you ever get in a situation like that again, call us. No questions asked." Kendra winked.

Lacie laughed. "I'll remember that, but I'll try not to be as clueless as a teenager in the future."

"Did Quinn take you home?"

"No." She blew out a sigh. "But he kept me from getting hit on. He *said* he was looking for one of his employees. And the guy did show up later."

"Quinn told me he hadn't drank a drop since our encounter. That was over two years ago; he was going through some stuff then."

When Lacie had been reeling from Mel's death and bringing Max into the world alone. She and Quinn had traversed a valley almost at the same time. What had happened to him?

She'd love to ask but knew Kendra wouldn't tell her.

Kendra cleared her throat. "How come you're so interested? Is he an old flame?"

"No." The word wrenched from her. Mel was the only flame she'd ever had. "We graduated together. That's all. But he offered me a part-time job teaching kids to ride."

"Are you going to take it?"

"I haven't decided."

"I don't mean to get personal, but are you okay on money? You know Stetson and I…"

"I don't need the money, but I loved teaching kids to ride and working with horses. I miss it."

Danielle let out a contented sigh. Kendra snuggled her closer.

Lacie didn't know what she'd do if she had to leave Max every day to work a forty-hour week. Especially when he'd

only been a baby. No wonder Kendra wanted to spend every spare moment with her daughter.

"Have you thought about quitting work?" Lacie chewed on the corner of her lip. "Or at least going part time like Rayna? Or maybe even starting your own photography studio?"

"I'm giving my notice tomorrow. Somehow, my career isn't that important anymore."

This from the woman who used to breathe photography?

"Something's going on. I'm a good listener."

Kendra's chin quivered. She hid most of her face in Danielle's neck. "Lynn and her family are moving back."

Lacie's heart sank.

"Lynn was seventeen, pregnant, and unmarried. And she was one of the good girls. She got taken in by the wrong guy." Kendra swiped a tear away. "You know Trent, the guy with all the tattoos?"

"He's Danielle's father?"

Kendra nodded. "Trent wasn't a Christian then. Lynn's dad was a deacon, and they were so embarrassed, they moved away. They hoped to move back some day. And we hoped so, too, but they were afraid if they returned, people might figure it out. So they stayed put.

"Once they decided to give up the baby for adoption, Stetson and I wanted to take her. We loved Lynn and felt like our decision would ease their minds."

Lacie touched Danielle's silky hair. "You're afraid once she gets a load of this little keeper, she'll change her mind."

"I feel like such a traitor." Kendra's hand trembled as she continued to pat Danielle's back. "I'm the youth director's wife, and I love Lynn, but now I want her to stay away from Danielle. And Trent, too." Her voice shook. "He knew Lynn was pregnant, but not that we were the adoptive parents. It might be my imagination, but I've caught him staring at Danielle lately."

"You're not a traitor." Lacie patted her arm. "You eased

Lynn's mind and gave Danielle a loving home. And if Trent knows, maybe he's grateful to you."

"I hope so."

"I'll pray so. I hate to leave you upset"—Lacie stood— "but, I better git. Left Max playing at Rayna's."

"I'm fine. We'll be fine."

She gave Kendra a quick squeeze and stepped off the porch.

Oh Lord, please let this little happy family stay intact. She mounted Copper, waved, and trotted the horse down the long drive. But when she got to the end, she turned away from Clay's ranch and toward Quinn's.

Clip-clop, clip-clop. The unmistakable sound of horse hooves on pavement. Quinn rounded the house from checking on the new colt. He shielded his eyes from the sun's glare and looked toward the road. A sorrel horse, its mane and tail slightly lighter than its coppery coat. The blond rider reined the horse into his long drive, Texas dust trailing behind.

Suspiciously similar to Lacie. His breath froze in his lungs.

The rider drew closer. Rhinestones glistened on her jacket, belt, and boots. Her red blouse matched her lips. It was Lacie. No—the sun had cooked his brain. Causing hallucinations.

"Nice day, huh?" The hallucination spoke, reined the horse to a halt, and swung down from her mount. Rhinestones lined the back pockets of her jeans, too.

He caught a whiff of haunting perfume. Sweet Honesty. His mom had sold Avon for years and filled lots of orders for Lacie's mom. Lacie had worn the fragrance since high school. The apparition was real. "What brings you by?"

"That job you mentioned."

Chapter 5

Quinn's heart pounded in his ears. Tell her he'd already hired someone. Push her away. He was no good for her. But how could he help her if he didn't spend time with her? "It's still open. You interested?"

"I loved working with kids." Her blue eyes shone. "I miss it and want to get back in it."

"I can call the folks who asked about lessons and set some up for you. Any time of day better for you? I don't want to cut into your time with Max."

"I'm thinking during his nap time—midday. But let me make a few arrangements, and I'll get back with you." She crossed her arms just above her tiny waist. "I'm definitely interested."

His heart dissolved to mush. If only she were talking about being interested in him. But that could never be. "I'll be waiting."

"If I take the job, would you mind if I boarded Copper here and maybe practiced some barrels? I'd pay you."

"Not necessary." He lowered his hat, hoping she couldn't see in his eyes what she did to him. "You can board her and practice here, even if you don't take the job."

"No, I insist on paying. Clay's arena is really busy, and he won't let me pay him, so I don't ride her much because I feel like I'm costing him."

"If it makes you feel better to pay, I reckon I could accept a small fee. I'd love to see you run barrels again." He remembered her barrel-queen days well. A tiny porcelain doll riding her steed like it was part of her, blond hair streaming out behind. A vision on horseback.

"Good. I'll get back with you. And thanks." She mounted her horse in one smooth motion then rode away.

He didn't breathe properly for a full five minutes.

His cell rang—breaking the spell of her perfume he could still smell.

"Hey Quinn. It's Rayna. We're having a trail ride and picnic next Saturday evening. We'd love for you to come. Kendra and Stetson are coming—you met them the other night—plus a few couples from church, and Lacie."

The last name on the list was all he needed to hear. Turn her down. Turn her down. But he couldn't. Lacie was like a drug, and he couldn't stay away.

Even if she could never be his. He had to keep a tight rein on his heart.

"Sure, I'll be there. Thanks for asking."

Lacie helped Max climb the training-arena fence. Positioning herself behind him in case he fell, she propped the toe of her boot on the bottom rail. This used to be her arena.

The new teacher, in her early twenties, led the small boy on horseback round and round. Dust flew with each hoof beat. She was good with the horse and the boy. Plenty of patience.

"Go horsey. Go." Max cheered.

"*Shh*. We can't disturb them. He's learning to ride."

Max watched intently.

"Trish does a great job," Clay whispered, standing behind her. "But I wish I could hire you back."

Max forgot all about the horse. "Cway." He reached for Clay.

"How's my favorite cowpoke?" Clay scooped him up.

"That boy's learning to ride horsey." Max pointed.

"He sure is." Clay propped Max on the fence's top rail, holding him secure.

"What do you think of"—her voice caught—"Quinn Remington?"

"Seems like an all right guy."

"He was always nice in high school. But he's different." She shoved her hands in her pockets. "It's like he's got the weight of the world and a few extra galaxies on him."

"I think something happened that knocked the stuffing out of him, and he's in that 'not worthy to be a Christian' mode folks fall into. I've been inviting him to church though." Clay raised an is-there-something-going-on brow. "Why?"

"Nothing like you're thinking. He wants me to teach kids to ride at his ranch."

"You should do it. I bet Rayna could help you with this little guy."

"I don't know."

"Even moms need some *me* time. And you don't take enough."

"It's just—" She sighed.

"What's going on, Lace?"

"I think…" She lowered her voice, not wanting to admit the words. But needing to confess. To herself. And Mel. "I'm attracted to him. I can't believe I said that out loud." Her eyes squeezed shut.

Clay grinned. "That's good, sweetheart. That means you're coming to life again."

"But—" A tidal wave in her chest cut her words off. Oh

Mel. How could she betray him by thinking about another man? She twisted the wedding rings, still on her finger.

"It's been two and a half years. You're young, and Mel would want you to be happy."

"Maybe I'm just lonely."

"Mel wouldn't want you to be lonely. And maybe nothing'll happen with Quinn. But it's time to start entertaining the possibility."

Lacie wagged her finger at him. "If you tell Rayna, I'll personally tan your hide. She's already having matchmaking ideas."

"Not a word. I'll even try to rein her in for you."

"*Try* is right." She rolled her eyes. "Since you finally convinced her *happily ever after* really happens, she wants to make sure everybody gets one."

Max sagged against Clay, his eyelids heavy.

"Come on, snookums." Lacie reached for him. "It's time for your nap."

"Me no need nap." He strained away from her with every inch of his two-year-old body.

"You always do what your mama says. Makes life easier, trust me." Clay scooped Max down to her. "Snookums? I think this little guy needs some male influence in his life."

She laughed. "I think he gets plenty of man vibes with you, your dad, and the ranch hands. Way more than enough."

"You may be right, but no more snookums. Cowpoke, partner, wrangler—stuff like that."

He dropped a kiss on the top of her head and gave her a quick squeeze.

She turned toward the ranch house. Clay loved Mel as much as she did. If Clay didn't think her horrible for being attracted to Quinn, maybe Mel wouldn't either. What if there were windows in heaven? Would her tentative steps toward a future without him make him sad, or would he cheer her on?

* * *

Quinn stared at the pink and lavender streaks the sunset painted above the trees. Numerous horses grazed, tied to hitching posts surrounding a large clearing in the woods. Permanent wooden benches provided seating, and a sun-bleached table held the food.

Lacie seemed surprised when he arrived. Reckon Rayna hadn't told her she'd invited him to their picnic. Would she have come if she'd known? Maybe. At least she was considering the job offer.

"Sorry for the heat, everyone." Rayna handed her empty plate to Clay. "We probably should've held this inside, but I'm so sick of being stuck in the house."

"Rayna's got cabin fever, literally." Clay circled the gathering with a trash bag. "She wanted some fresh air—make that hot air. Maybe I'll build a pavilion."

"It's not too bad with the shade. And the sun's going down." Lacie shielded her eyes and checked the horizon.

Quinn forced his gaze away from her. Especially from her tanned legs topped by cutoff blue jeans. Come on sun, go on down. Quick. Why had he chosen the bench directly across from her with a mere five feet separating them?

Heat seared his heart and his lungs. He sure could use a fan.

Two baby girls and a toddler boy captivated the adults sitting around in canvas folding chairs. The redhead girl obviously belonged to Clay and Rayna. What was her name? Kayla—yeah that's it. Danielle was Kendra and Stetson's. If he hadn't known she was adopted, he sure couldn't have told by the love they lavished on her.

"Stay away from the horses." Lacie cautioned as Max wandered out of her range.

"Big." The boy traveled a large circle, well away from the horses.

Blond hair, dark eyes. A real rounder, wearing shorts that

stopped just above a tiny pair of cowboy boots. He stared at Quinn's boots then took sure-footed steps right up to him.

"Howdy, partner. Not shy, are you?" Quinn reached for the tyke.

Lacie swooped in from nowhere and scooped up the boy. "Let's get you a drink."

"He wasn't bothering me. I love kids."

"He loves men," she whispered. "I try not to let him get attached to anyone who won't be a part of his life." She scurried away from him and over to the table.

Firmly put in his place.

Exactly why had he come?

The hair along the back of his neck prickled. He caught Stetson's glare.

Stetson's gaze darted away.

No, Quinn didn't belong in this gathering. Lacie didn't want him here. Stetson didn't want him here. Kendra didn't want him here. If only they'd clue Rayna in, so she'd stop inviting him.

Why hadn't he mustered up the backbone to refuse and stay away from Lacie? If only he'd known Mel Gentry's widow was the woman he'd fallen for back in high school. The woman he'd never forgotten.

Rayna repositioned Kayla in her lap. "So, Lacie, since we got our babysitting details worked out, are you going to take the job Quinn offered you?"

Quinn's ears perked up.

"I think so."

"Good. I know you loved your job at the ranch, and I wish we could hire you back. But I guess we'll have to let Quinn have you."

Lacie's hand flew to her heart.

His gaze held hers. If only he could have her. He'd spend the rest of his days making up for the hurt he'd caused her. "When you coming to work?"

"Whenever you get me some riders to teach. Afternoons are best. Maybe three days a week."

"I'll get on it and let you know." No turning back now. Three days a week with Lacie working at his ranch. So close. But they could never span the gulf of Mel Gentry's death standing between them.

A text message alert sounded on someone's cell. Rayna dug in her pocket. "Gabby's in labor."

"Sorry to be bad hosts, but sounds like we'd better get to the hospital." Clay unhitched his and Rayna's horses.

"I wanna go." Kendra stood and scooped up her daughter.

Anticipation glowed in Lacie's eyes. "Me, too."

If only he could see her eyes light up over him. "Y'all go on. I'll pack what's left and take it back to the ranch house fridge before I leave."

First day, last student. Lacie led the white-and-brown-splotched Pinto around the arena. "There, that's it. You're getting it. Sit up tall."

Six-year-old Tawny gradually relaxed astride the horse. "Look Daddy, look."

"You did great. That's it for today." Lacie stopped the horse and held her steady near the child's father while Tawny climbed down.

"You looked like a natural up there," Mr. Masters said.

"Can I come back, Daddy? Please."

"Sounds like we're setting up a weekly lesson."

"Great." Lacie smiled. "I'll put her on the schedule. Same time?"

"Please." He took his daughter's hand.

The little girl chattered all the way to the parking lot.

Lacie undid the girth, folded the right stirrup and straps up onto the seat so they wouldn't hit the horse, and swung the saddle down from her back.

"I planned to take care of that." Quinn's voice came from behind her. "This thing's as big as you are."

"I've been saddling and unsaddling horses since I was twelve. I can handle it."

"Well around here, you don't have to." He grabbed the saddle from her. "How'd your first day go?"

"I had fun." Her insides did a little somersault. "The Masters girl wants weekly lessons. Same time."

"Great. That's three students for each day you teach. I watched you from the kitchen window. You're really good. With the kids and with the horse."

"Patience." She smiled. "It's the secret to both."

Music played, and Quinn dug a cell phone from his pocket. "Desperado." A hauntingly lonely song to choose for a ringtone.

"Hello?" He stared in the distance, listening to the caller.

While he was distracted, Lacie looked him over. His pale eyes were a striking contrast to his sun-darkened skin and almost-black hair. Lines and contours honed his bone structure. Strong, rugged, and hard working. Handsome, yet gentle.

"I appreciate the offer, but I don't announce anymore." He lowered the brim of his hat. "No. If I think of anyone, I'll let you know." He slid the phone closed but turned his back on her.

Awkward silence hung on the breeze. He led the horse toward the barn.

She should go. Instead, she trailed behind him. "I always thought announcing a rodeo would be fun."

"I had my fill of it." His voice was gruff.

The raw emotion in his tone put a lump in her throat. What did he have against the rodeo? Had he fallen in love with a cowgirl? Did she break his heart? Why else would a handsome man like Quinn be alone? He must be pining over some lost love.

"I love the Stockyards. At first, after Mel died, I felt closest

to him at the rodeo. Somehow, it was comforting." Why did she tell him that? She shoved her hands in her back pockets.

"And now?"

"Even with Clay retired, I still love going. I reckon I go to cheer Stetson on." She hurried ahead of him to open the gate. "Most of Mel and Clay's bunch have moved on or retired, so I don't know many of the Stockyards' cowboys anymore, but I'm there every Friday and Saturday night. I guess it's in my blood."

Here she was rattling on, and he wouldn't even look at her.

"I'd best be going. I told Rayna I'd be back by five."

"Thanks for coming over today." Finally he faced her. "You really were great with the kids."

"I guess I'll see you Wednesday."

"See you then." He led the horse to its stall.

Wow. Whatever was eating him was chowing down.

Quinn harrumphed a huge sigh, punched his pillow, and closed his eyes. His mind drifted.

Dust flew as the cowboy hit the dirt—head first. The bronc stopped bucking and headed for the gate. But Mel Gentry didn't move.

Quinn opened his eyes. Would he ever go a whole day without that vision? It always struck when he got still, when the house was quiet with no distractions. No matter how late he stayed up. No matter how tired he was.

Now that he knew Lacie had been there that night—had witnessed her husband's death—his fully awake nightmare had a new twist—Lacie's terror-riddled face in the crowd.

He rolled onto his side, facing the window. Moonlight washed the room with its eerie glow.

And yet Lacie was doing better than he was. Because the guilt didn't lie at her feet. It lay squarely at Quinn's.

How could she still go to the rodeo? He hadn't stepped foot near an arena since Mel's death.

But Lacie had faced her demons. She was moving on. Sadness still lurked in her eyes, but so did determination. Determination to be strong for her son.

He rolled over again.

Maybe if he went to the rodeo, the nightmare would go away. Maybe he could replace it with new images—of cowboys riding until the buzzer sounded, jumping nimbly from their mounts and exiting the arena.

He felt for the remote on his nightstand. Bright-blue digital numbers on the clock glowed 3:12 a.m. He clicked on the TV. Something lighthearted. TV Land? He clicked until he found the channel. Soft voices. A classic sitcom.

He closed his eyes.

If only life came with a laugh track.

Lacie sat next to Kendra in the box seats. Countless times Mel had kissed her here before heading to the chutes.

The huge tractor parked in the middle of the arena revved to life, signaling the beginning of the rodeo. Fans claimed seats in a steady stream. Cowtown Coliseum, her second home.

"Kendra, I need a favor." Wyatt Marshall squatted beside them, holding his infant daughter.

"Hey cutie." Lacie's arms ached to hold her, as they had a few weeks ago at the hospital when Gabby brought a new baby boy into the world.

"Thanks." Wyatt grinned.

Her cheeks warmed. "I meant—"

"I know. Just joshing with you. My sister couldn't keep Hannah tonight."

"Can I hold her?" Lacie reached for the baby. Lavender-scented shampoo and sweet baby smell took her back to when Max was so tiny. "What a sweetie. How old is she now?"

"Eleven months." Wyatt swung a diaper bag off his shoulder and sat it between them. "I owe you gals a million. I'm

in the second round of bulls, so it'll be a while, but I'll come get her as soon as my ride's over."

"You may have a fight on your hands." Lacie snuggled the baby close.

"Nobody'll ever get my girl from me." He gently cupped the back of his daughter's head with a calloused hand then swaggered toward the bucking chutes.

"I'm so proud of him." Kendra stuffed the diaper bag under her metal folding chair. "Who'd have ever thought he'd make such a great dad? A single dad at that?"

"Does Natalie ever have anything to do with her?"

"No. After Wyatt managed to change her mind about abortion, Natalie signed her rights over to him and left town soon after Hannah's birth."

"How could a mother give up her child and cut all ties? I just don't understand it."

Kendra's shoulders sagged.

Oh to get those words back. Lacie closed her eyes. "I'm sorry." What else could she say? "Open mouth, insert foot. Wanna go get something to drink?"

"No. It's starting anyway."

"Ladies and gentlemen. Welcome to the Cowtown Coliseum, home of the first indoor rodeo. Fasten your seatbelts; it's gonna be a bumpy ride."

She knew that voice. Quinn.

Kendra shielded her eyes from the spotlights and scanned the announcer's booth.

"I didn't know Quinn was the new announcer."

"Me, either." She'd distinctly heard him turn down the offer, and she hadn't realized his offer came from Cowtown.

The music started, and Hannah jumped. Her little face grew red, and she let out a wail.

Lacie stood. "I think I'll go get that drink. I'm not sure blaring music is so good for baby ears anyway." She headed to the lobby, soothing the baby as she went.

And besides, Quinn had managed to invade her turf once more. She couldn't seem to get away from him.

Quinn climbed down the stairs from the announcer's booth. When he'd arrived, one glimpse of the arena and he'd felt like his chest would explode. But the night had gone well. Broncs and bulls. Some riders made the buzzer; some fell. But no dead cowboys.

He rounded the arena and exited into the private lobby where dozens of cowboys filed out after a hard night's ride.

Lacie. His steps faltered. Blond, delicate, and beautiful. She held the tiny hands of a baby, walking the child between her feet. A baby too small to be Max. Her gaze met his.

Come on feet, work. He walked toward her, trying for casual. "Who we got here?"

"This is Hannah. Isn't she a doll?"

"There's my baby girl." A sandy-haired man reached for the baby and smiled at Lacie. "Was she good?"

"Very good, but the music bothered her, so we stayed in the lobby and practiced walking most of the time."

The man frowned. "I made you miss the rodeo."

"It's okay. This little angel was worth it."

"I owe you one, Lacie. Don't know what I'd have done without you." He kissed Lacie's cheek. "This single father stuff is tough sometimes. But well worth it."

Something in Quinn's chest tightened. Was this single dad on the prowl for a mommy for his little girl? Had he set his sights on Lacie?

Chapter 6

Quinn's mouth went dry.

"This is Wyatt Marshall. A friend," Lacie added. "Wyatt, Quinn Remington. We graduated high school together."

"The new backup announcer." Wyatt offered his hand.

Take the baby and waylay the man. Instead, Quinn gripped Wyatt's hand. "That's me."

"Glad to have you on board. You did a fine job tonight."

Straggling competitors, surrounded by well wishers, trickled through the lobby, filling it with booming conversation and laughter.

"Thanks," Quinn shouted over the ruckus. At least the new man in Lacie's life was nice. What idiot would think she was unattached, as lovely and sweet as she was? Men would naturally herd around her.

Was this guy worthy of her? Or was he looking for someone to make his single fatherhood easier? Was he using Lacie to shirk his responsibilities?

He couldn't stand around and watch her with her *friend*.

Not for another second. "See you around." He hurried to the exit, his heart pounding in his ears.

At least September was slightly cooler. Lacie led her last student around the arena at Quinn's. He was everywhere she went. Every time she turned around at Clay and Rayna's ranch, at the job she didn't even need, and now announcing rodeos at Cowtown Coliseum. She had to quit her job. Before her lonely heart got too accustomed to him.

That's what it was—loneliness that made her heart giddy when she saw him, that made her anticipate their next meeting. Loneliness—and he made her feel safe. A safe man was too much for her lonely heart to deal with. Especially since something had stalled his walk with the Lord.

Her grip tightened on the horse's rein.

But this was her last student for the day, and she hadn't seen Quinn at all. *Stop focusing on him, and focus on the boy on the horse.*

"Okay, you're doing great."

At fifteen, the boy was her oldest student. Huge splashes of mottled red stained his cheeks if she even looked in his direction. He'd been terrified to even get near the placid horse at first. But she'd let him feed Trigger a carrot, and they'd made fast friends.

"You want to take the reins?"

"No, ma'am." The answer came quick. He glanced at his father, standing outside the arena. "In fact, I think I'd like to get off now."

"You've still got another twenty minutes."

"I want off."

"All right. I'll hold her steady. Dismount on her left. Swing your right leg up, and climb down backward."

The boy followed her instructions without any problem and exited the arena with a mumbled "thanks."

His father watched him walk to the truck. "You're a very gifted trainer, Miss Gentry."

"I won't charge you for the full hour."

"It's well worth it. He hasn't been on a horse since he fell off when he was six. This is only his second lesson, and you got him on."

Something warmed inside her. She'd helped her student. It had been so long since she'd felt the glow of accomplishment. "I don't want to hurt your feelings, but I think he'd do even better if you didn't stick around to watch."

"Not a problem. I'll drop him off next lesson and find something to do for an hour. I want him to stop being afraid. Whatever it takes. He loves horses, but after that one experience, I never could get him to ride again. I'm so glad we found you."

"Me, too." She smiled. So much for quitting her job. "See you next week."

He waved and jogged to his truck.

If Quinn would stay away, she could do this job she loved.

She got a firm hold on the horse's reins, opened the gate, and walked the horse to the boarding stables, where the groomer took over.

A few stalls down she caught a glimpse of Copper stomping the dust, obviously wanting out of her daytime home. Probably eighteen minutes left. She could get in a nice ride.

"Want me to saddle her for you?" Quinn's voice called from the next stall.

Lacie jumped. "Quinn Remington, I didn't know you were anywhere around."

"Sorry I startled you."

The horse in his stall already wore a saddle and bridle. Ready to go.

Oh please, don't let him be getting ready for a ride. She could pet her horse and leave, but Copper ached for a ride as much as she did.

"I can saddle her." Lacie gently laid a quilted pad on her mare's back and lifted the saddle off its stand. Admittedly, it took all her strength to hoist it up onto Copper's back, but she did it, just as she had thousands of times. She slid the bridle over the horse's head and fastened it in place.

"Care if I join you?"

With every fiber in my being. "Of course not. But I don't have long." She led Copper out just as Quinn rode a gray-and-white-spattered Appaloosa out of his stall.

"Does Copper run barrels?"

"Like nobody's business. Clay trained her and used her for folks training for barrels."

"Wanna see what she can do?"

Something fluttered in her chest. She hadn't run barrels in years. "There's not enough time."

"Come on, the barrels are already set up. We're talking a matter of seconds here."

"Okay." It didn't take much to convince her.

Quinn urged his horse to a trot.

Lacie mounted Copper and followed him around the huge boarding stables.

He opened the center gate.

Quivering with anticipation, Copper pranced in the arena.

Lacie positioned the horse in line with the middle barrel. "I haven't done this in a good five years. But you have, Copper. *Yah!*" She dug both heels in Copper's sides.

The horse surged forward, slowed to make a tight line around the barrel, and then sped to the next. Horse and rider, one fluid motion, as if they'd been together for years. Warmth spread through Lacie; she couldn't stop smiling.

Copper rounded the last barrel and sped to the alley.

Mel whooped.

Giddy, Lacie turned to face him.

But it was Quinn, not Mel.

Her smile melted.

"Fifteen–five. Thirteen or fourteen seconds is usually a winning score. You sure you haven't been practicing?"

"If we'd been practicing, it would've been *thirteen–five*." She patted Copper. "Good girl."

She pointed her mare toward the barn.

"Hey, aren't we going on a ride?"

Flee—turn Copper over to the groomer and fly back to the ranch as quick as she could. But Copper loved to run. It would be cruel to take her best friend for one barrel run and then lock her up until the riding finished for the day, when she'd be free to roam and graze the pastures.

"A short one, I guess." She checked her watch and aimed Copper to the riding trail.

Copper whinnied her appreciation.

Quinn stole glances at her as they rode.

He'd loved watching her dash around those barrels, just as she had at eighteen. The last ten years had melted away for him.

And she'd smiled the first genuine smile he'd seen from her, other than when she was with Max.

But then she'd gone all stiff. And he'd remembered Mel.

The trail narrowed, with moss-draped live oaks creating a canopy above them. A chorus of birds twittered and called to each other.

"You really should compete at the Stockyards. It's obvious you still love barrel racing."

"I might."

"I'll even pay your fee to get you started." He rode side by side with her, within touching distance of one another.

"I can pay my own fee."

"I know you can, but I'm figuring you won't. So I—"

"Can we drop it?" Her tone went tight, cold.

"Sorry. I'm only trying to encourage you. Sorry if I stepped on your toes."

"I'm sorry. I didn't mean to snap at you. I appreciate the encouragement. It's just… Mel was the last person to encourage me to get back into barrel racing. He just about had me talked into it, and then I got pregnant. And then…"

A knot lodged in Quinn's throat. *And then I killed him.* "I'm sorry."

"Me, too. I don't know if I can do it without him cheering me on. I mean, we met at a rodeo, and even before our first date, he cheered me on."

Quinn let her sadness sink into his soul. "I know it would never be the same, but I'd love to cheer you on."

He heard her sharp intake of breath, and she reined her horse to a stop.

"Course I'd have to be neutral if I announced, but Kendra would cheer you on. And Wyatt." He forced the name out. "Clay and Rayna might even come to watch you."

"I'll think about it." She turned Copper around. "I really have to get back now. I need to get home to Max."

If only he could shore up the holes in her soul.

Lacie let Copper rest and glanced toward the house. She wanted Quinn to leave her alone, but she wanted to see him. He made her crazy. How had this happened? This was only her third week of working for him.

Her heart hammered in her chest.

Did she have feelings for him? Or was she lonely and reading too much into it because he was familiar? Comfortable. But nothing about him made her comfortable. Safe, but not comfortable.

One more run. She positioned Copper in line with the first barrel and felt the horse's body tense. "*Yah!*"

She clicked the stopwatch on the chain around her neck as the horse sailed into action. With precise turns, the mare rounded each barrel and bolted to the gate. As she crossed

the line, Lacie clicked the stopwatch. Fourteen–five. Not bad. They'd shaved off an entire second.

"Good girl." She patted her horse and swung down from the saddle. "That's enough for the day."

She glanced toward the house one more time and led Copper out of the arena and to the stables.

Her cell rang, and she dug it from her pocket.

"Lacie." Her mother's soothing voice washed over her frayed nerves. "Are you settled enough for me and your father to come up for a visit?"

"Perfect timing, I've been meaning to call you." Family. Exactly what she needed to get her mind off Quinn. She patted Copper. "When are y'all coming?"

"Got any plans next weekend?"

"I don't. And I might have a surprise for you Friday night."

The only problem was—if she surprised them, she'd have to deal with Quinn's presence.

Who was she talking to? Wyatt? She sure smiled a lot.

From his bedroom window, Quinn had watched Lacie charge Copper around the barrels. And he'd spent the last three hours before that staring out his kitchen window as she worked with students. She'd turned him into a stalker.

If he gave her some space, she'd be more comfortable and focused. And maybe he'd be more comfortable and focused on finding ways to help her. But he couldn't take his eyes off her.

She twisted him in knots, those complicated Boy Scout knots he'd had so much trouble with.

She led the horse around the stables, and he went into the living room, making a point to stay away from the windows. He was here to help her. But what had he done for her? He'd given her a job and encouraged her to barrel race. That's all. He wasn't here to spy on her—or fall more deeply in love with her.

A knock sounded at the door.

He hurried to answer and caught a glimpse through the glass. Lacie. On his porch. To see him. His heart did a silly, giddy dance as he swung the door open.

Her windblown hair tumbled out of her ponytail. Damp strands hung around her face. His hand ached to tuck them behind her ears, trace the soft line of her jaw with his fingertips. His hand clenched.

"Hey. Did you see me run barrels? I thought you might've happened by those windows at the back of the house."

"I noticed one run." One of the biggest lies he'd ever told, but he couldn't admit he'd camped out in his bedroom to watch every run.

"Good." She smiled. "How did my form look?"

"Beautiful." Oh. She meant her form on the horse. "I mean—you ride like you're part of the horse. You always have."

"I tried to time myself. Kind of hard to do while riding, but I got 14:5 once."

He'd timed 13:43. "The run I saw looked faster."

"Really?" She did a little excited bounce. "My folks are coming to visit this weekend. I'm thinking I might compete at the Stockyards Friday and surprise them. Daddy always loved to watch me compete."

"I think you should do it. You're ready."

"You really think so?" The wind blew a strand of hair across her face.

His fingers itched to smooth it away. Incapable of thought except for how beautiful she was, he barely hung onto the conversation. "I think so."

She threw her arms around him. "Me, too. Thanks for encouraging me."

His arms encircled her, never wanting to let go. For ten long years, he'd wanted to hold her like this. Well not quite like this. But it would do.

She pushed away, backed up. A confused frown marred her features. "I'd better get home." She ran to her SUV.

A whole week had passed, and that hug still haunted Lacie.

She took a couple of deep breaths, inhaling manure fragrance galore. She hadn't been behind the gate in Cowtown Coliseum in over five years. And never on a horse. Copper's hide danced with nervous energy. They were both a mess.

She and her parents had missed the first round of bulls, and by the time they'd arrived, Quinn was already announcing. Barrel racing came next then the final round of bulls.

Nerves from listening to Quinn's voice for two hours collided with nerves over the coming event and turned her into one big jumble.

He'd made himself scarce during her riding lessons this week, and she was glad. If only she could get through the rest of the evening without running into him. Especially with Mama and Daddy in tow.

They thought she'd gone to get drinks. She grinned. She'd love to see Daddy's face when Quinn announced her name.

Her ride was next.

"Next up, Lacie Gentrrryyyy," Quinn echoed her name. "I've had the privilege of watching this little lady's practice runs. This former homecoming queen and Miss Rodeo Texas Teen tears the arena up. Hold on to your hats, cowboys."

Lacie's cheeks burned by the time he finished his introduction. So much for him remaining neutral. Copper pranced down the center alley into the arena.

"*Yah!*" Lacie hunkered low, her body in sync with Copper's. Each turn perfect—fast and tight. It was a good ride. She could feel it. Last barrel. Copper made the turn and charged back to the center alley.

"Thirteen–fifty-two. Didn't I tell you? Boy howdy, that was some ride." Still not sounding very neutral up there.

Lacie swung down from Copper and hugged her neck. "You did great. We just might place in this thing."

Quinn wound up the announcements quick as he could after the final round of bulls and hurried down from his booth. She was probably gone by now, but maybe he could get a glimpse of her.

He'd tried to keep his distance after that spontaneous hug she'd given him. His heart couldn't handle touching her, but he needed to at least see her.

He cut through to the rear lobby. And there she was, a huge smile on her face, surrounded by fans. Rayna and Clay, Kendra and Stetson, and her folks and Star. He hung back, and no one noticed him.

Wyatt joined the gathering.

Something boiled inside Quinn.

"Wyatt Marshall, meet my parents and my sister, Star."

Wyatt's gaze lingered on Star a little too long. What a loser. Checking out his girlfriend's sister right out in the open.

Star was a dark-haired version of Lacie. Beautiful, but not as delicate and lovely as Lacie, at least in Quinn's opinion.

"We should've known you were a rodeo queen the first time we got a load of you." Wyatt winked at Lacie.

Winked at her.

Chapter 7

Quinn's fists clenched.

Lacie rolled her eyes. "That was a lifetime ago."

"Well you still got the horsemanship part down pat. And the beauty, too, I'd say"—Rayna hugged her—"Miss From-Out-of-Nowhere Second Place."

"I can't believe you never told us you were homecoming queen." Kendra shook her head. "And a barrel queen for that matter."

A cluster of cowboys herded through, shouting, guffawing, and interrupting for a moment.

Wyatt grabbed the opportunity to move closer to Lacie, and the lobby cleared. "Still is. On both counts in my book. Mel would be real proud of you." He squeezed her shoulder. "So how long you folks staying?"

Checking out her sister and invoking her husband's name to warm up to her. This guy was some piece of work.

"We're leaving Monday morning," Lacie's dad answered.

"Maybe I'll see y'all in church tomorrow. Maybe even at Moms." Wyatt tipped his hat and headed for the exit.

Quinn closed his eyes. At least Wyatt went to church. Which was more than Quinn did these days. But if Lacie's relationship with Wyatt was close enough that she visited his mom with him, why was he checking out her sister? What had Lacie gotten herself into with this guy?

At least Lacie's mom and dad were here, and he didn't have to watch her leave with Wyatt.

"Mom's." Star's left eyebrow arched. "Did he invite us to his mother's?"

"No. Moms on Main. It's a restaurant where lots of our church folks eat lunch after morning services."

Maybe they weren't so serious after all. The boil in his chest slowed to a simmer.

Lacie's mom caught sight of him. "Quinn Remington."

Busted. He joined the celebration.

She hugged him. "Lacie told us that was you announcing up there."

"Mrs. Maxwell. Nice seeing you again."

"You can drop the Mrs. Maxwell." She patted his arm. "Just call me Karen."

"And I'm Gerald." Lacie's dad shook his hand.

"I'm not sure I can. My mama would tan my hide."

Mrs. Maxwell laughed. "We're all adults. No need for such formalities. Gerald and I have always thought the world of you and your family."

Lacie grimaced.

"Same here."

"Lacie told us you live here now." Gerald kept pumping his hand. "I'm pleased to know Lacie has such good neighbors and friends."

"Dad. Let go," Lacie whispered.

Gerald looked at their hands as if he hadn't realized they were still clasped and pulled his away.

Rayna giggled, and Lacie shot her a glare. Rayna meandered to the exit with Lacie's other friends.

Say something. Fill in the awkward silence. "I try to be neighborly. Speaking of which, I can load up Copper in my trailer and take her back to my ranch."

"I can handle it." Lacie was quick as ever to decline his help.

"There's no need for you to take her, when I'm going there anyway."

"Quinn boards Copper for you?" Mrs. Maxwell grinned. "I thought she was at Clay's ranch."

"She was. But his arena is always busy, and I've been working with her on barrels, so I moved her to Quinn's."

"Well he's right then. It doesn't make sense for you to take Copper—unless y'all had a date or something."

Lacie's mouth opened. And closed.

Stunned, Quinn couldn't help her out. Did they not know about her and Wyatt?

"We're not dating." Lacie's tone could've cut glass. "Besides, it's almost midnight."

"I'll help Lacie get Copper loaded, and then y'all can go on without having to stop at my place."

"Good idea." Lacie nudged her mom toward the exit. "Y'all go wait in the SUV and I'll be right there."

Maybe the mid-September air outside hadn't cooled yet. Or maybe it was only the conversation that made the rear lobby feel stuffy and Lacie's temperature rise. "I'm sorry about my mom."

"Don't apologize for her. She's a lovely lady. I always thought so."

"She is." Lacie strode toward the exit. "But sometimes, I'd like to crawl in a hole at the stuff she comes up with."

"She wants you to be happy. No harm in that."

"I wish she'd stop…"

"Trying to find you a new husband?"

She nodded.

"I'm just glad Wyatt had already left."

"Why?" She frowned.

"What she said might have bothered him. Shouldn't she point her matchmaking radar at him?"

"She shouldn't point her matchmaking radar anywhere." She stopped.

A bubble of hope swelled in his chest. "Aren't y'all an item?"

Lacie laughed.

"They don't know about him, do they?"

"There is no him. Wyatt recently became a Christian. He's a friend. That's all."

His mouth twitched, but he managed to squelch the smile.

"Why would you think we were… ?"

"A couple of weeks ago, here at the rodeo, y'all seemed kind of cozy. He kissed you on the cheek."

"He was a single father, desperate for a babysitter. He was just grateful. Kind of like when you encouraged me about barrels, and I…I hugged you. Because I was grateful for the encouragement."

So that's what it was. His chest deflated. But at least she wasn't seeing Wyatt.

"I'm not interested. In anyone." She twisted her wedding rings around her finger. "In my heart"—her voice caught—"I'm still married. I don't know why no one can understand that."

Her eyes glistened.

His arms ached to hold her. Let her cry it out on his shoulder.

"You go on and get your folks home. I'll take care of Copper."

She blinked several times. "Thanks," she said and strode away.

* * *

Lacie hadn't cried herself to sleep in a while. Until last night. She doused her swollen lids with cold water and took more time than usual with her makeup. Hopefully, her parents wouldn't be able to tell.

Fresh coffee aroma beckoned; she trudged to the small kitchen in her suite. Whoever invented the programmable coffee maker deserved to be a millionaire.

Mama and Daddy entered, greeted her, and each claimed a chair at the kitchen table.

She fixed their coffees the way they liked, set the cups in front of them, and then stirred sugar and hazelnut creamer into her own.

"We have news," Mama announced, her voice giddy.

"What?"

"We've decided to move to Denton." Daddy sipped his coffee.

"What?" Lacie squeaked.

"With you here and Star in Denton, your mother and I are lonely in San Antonio."

Having her parents near would be a blessing. Her heart warmed. She'd missed them. But Mama could matchmake even better living only twenty minutes away.

"But you've lived in San Antonio forever. In our house forever."

"It hasn't really been home since my two favorite girls left." Daddy's mug clattered on the table.

She knew exactly what he meant.

"The house is too big for the two of us." Mama shrugged. "We've been talking about downsizing anyway. We figure— why not downsize to Denton?"

"What if Star gets married again and moves to Florida? Are y'all gonna follow?"

Mama grinned. "Has she met someone?"

"In Florida?" Daddy scoffed. "Where did she meet someone from Florida?"

Lacie laughed. "She hasn't met anyone, as far as I know. But what if?"

"We'll cross that bridge when we get there."

One of Mama's favorite sayings.

"Families should be together." Daddy put his arm around her shoulders.

"We've missed over two years of Max's life already." Mama's voice cracked. "And he's growing so fast; we don't want to miss any more."

Guilt jabbed her. She was a heel, an absolute heel for worrying about Mama's matchmaking. She needed them. And Max did, too. She'd shown her independence since Mel's death, and she was tired. "When are y'all moving?"

"We already put our house up for sale." Mama clapped her hands. "So as soon as we find a place in Denton, we'll move. It'll be a whole new adventure."

The very thing Mama had always said when she and Star faced changes during their growing-up years. Whether it was school transfers, not making the basketball team, or making the cheering squad—it was all a whole new adventure. Tears pricked her eyes. Yes, having Mama and Daddy near would be a blessing.

"We were thinking you could move in with us." Mama's eyes sparkled.

"Max and I are fine here."

"But you can't live here forever."

"Exactly. We'll get a place of our own, because I'm an adult, and Max needs to see me taking care of us."

Daddy covered Mama's hand with his. "For the record, I told her not to ask you."

"I guess you'll want to stay in Aubrey anyway—close to Quinn."

Lacie's breath stalled. "Mama, I love you. But if you don't quit with the Quinn stuff, I'll toss you out on your ear."

"She's got your spirit, dear." Daddy grinned.

"Mommy," Max called from down the hallway.

Saved by the toddler.

Quinn swung his front door open.

Lacie stood, fist cocked in midknock, with Max, nearly half as big as she was, straddling her hip.

"I'm so sorry, but Kayla's sick, so Rayna can't keep Max. And Clay's mom and Kendra are both working today. I'm afraid I'll have to cancel, but if you'll give me my students' numbers, I'll call them."

Another opportunity to help her. "I can keep him."

She shook her head. "No. I couldn't do that."

"I'm great with kids and overly cautious where they're concerned. He'll be in great hands."

"But I—"

"I know." Don't let him get attached to anyone who won't be a part of his life. "But I'm your boss and neighbor, and I'm not planning on going anywhere. Even if you move, we run in the same circles. Seems me and Max are destined to be friends."

Max reached for him.

"See? We'll be fine."

Lacie kept her hold on her son. "But it's not time for lessons yet. I came early. We'll go back home. And I'm still not sure about this."

"Come on in. No sense in going back home for an hour. Max and I can get acquainted and put your mind at ease. I'll make coffee. And hot chocolate."

"Hot chocolate." Max squirmed away from Lacie.

She let go. "I guess we can stay."

"Good." Quinn ushered her in and closed the door. Thankfully, his housekeeper had come yesterday. The house was

neat and orderly. His jigsaw puzzle spread over the mat on his coffee table. He rolled one edge. "I'll get this out of the way."

"I love jigsaw puzzles," Lacie squealed. "I haven't done one since...since I left home. Daddy and I used to do them."

"My grandfather used to let me help him when I was a kid. So much of my business is done on the phone these days; I keep a puzzle going to occupy my mind and my hands."

She scanned the five-thousand-piece picture of wild mustangs running free. Her fingers twitched.

"Knock yourself out." He pointed to an empty section. "I've been trying to find that piece all morning."

Lacie studied the puzzle then tried three different pieces. The fourth piece she chose slipped into place.

"And you found it in two minutes."

Max poked the horsehead clasp on Quinn's bolo tie. "Horsey."

"You like that? It was my granddaddy's." Quinn lifted Max to sit on his shoulders. "Hold on partner, and we'll get that hot chocolate."

Lacie's mouth opened. She stood and reached for Max, looking like she might come undone at seeing him up so high.

"Don't worry. I've got him."

Max giggled.

A big sigh huffed out of her, but she sat down again.

She trusted him. With her son. "Be back in a jiff."

This was a mistake. Lacie slid another piece of the puzzle into place. She should retrieve Max and go home. It was one thing for her to get attached to Quinn. But letting Max get emotionally involved was an entirely different thing.

She'd already allowed him to love Clay. And since Kayla's birth, Clay needed to spend time with his own child, not hers.

Though Rayna and Clay were happy to include them in family gatherings, they weren't part of the family. And the

Warrens should be able to focus on their own family without feeling torn.

Another piece of the puzzle slid into place. She stood, intent on reclaiming her child, going home, and rescheduling her students. Movement outside the window caught her attention.

David Morris, her fifteen-year-old student. The one who'd been afraid to ride two lessons ago. Extremely early. She hurried outside.

Mr. Morris approached the porch. "Hello, Miss Gentry. David was so eager for his lesson, he wanted to come hang out until then. I told him I didn't think it was a good idea. We don't want to disturb your other students."

Enthusiasm shone in the boy's eyes. She couldn't cancel on him. She'd just have to be extra vigilant in the future with a backup babysitter. When Mama and Daddy relocated to Denton, it would give Lacie another option.

"That's fine, Mr. Morris. In fact, it might help David to watch my more experienced riders. If he can be very quiet, he can stay." She checked her watch. "And since I still owe y'all twenty minutes, we could get in a quick lesson before my first student arrives. Let me get things settled. Y'all go on out to the arena."

"I certainly don't want to inconvenience you, Miss Gentry."

"Please, call me Lacie. And it's not a problem. In fact, once I get out to the arena, you can go run errands if you want. I'll be right out." She stepped back inside.

"*Yee-haw.*" Quinn came back into the living room with Max clinging to one of his legs, and both feet on Quinn's cowboy boot. "We're getting along famously. Here's your coffee."

She grabbed the cup. "Max, let go. You'll scuff Mr. Quinn's boots."

"He's not hurting nothing. It was my idea."

"One of my students arrived early, so we're going to get

in some extra time." She downed a gulp of coffee, scalding her throat. Her eyes watered.

"Don't you worry your pretty little head. We'll be just fine. Won't we, partner?" Quinn scooped up Max and held him above his head.

Max giggled. The way he would have if Mel had gotten the chance to play baby airplane with him.

Her teeth sank into her lip until she tasted blood.

"Do you go to church?" Max asked.

Quinn cleared his throat. "Probably should."

"I want a prize."

"Now Max, that's not what church is about." She wagged a finger at him and reluctantly turned to Quinn. "His Sunday school teacher gives prizes when they bring a friend."

"Wanna come?" Max turned puppy-dog eyes on Quinn.

"We'll see, partner."

In adult speak, that meant probably not—another reason this was wrong. Allowing her son to become attached to a man who wouldn't even go to church. This had to be the last time Max spent time with Quinn. Especially alone. But right now, she didn't have an option.

Fresh from the shower, Quinn settled in his recliner. The sale barn always made it a long day, yet he loved it. Handpicking horses to buy and transporting them home made him feel alive. He did so much of his business on the phone, he often felt ranch bound.

The phone pealed next to him. He jumped and grabbed it.

"Mr. Quinn Remington?" asked an unfamiliar male voice.

"Yes."

"This is State Trooper William Ford."

Quinn's heart lodged in his throat. Lacie?

Chapter 8

"I'm sorry to report that Hank Andrews has been in a serious one-vehicle accident." Sympathy echoed in the officer's voice.

"Hank?" Quinn closed his eyes. Probably been drinking.

"We found one of your payroll stubs in the truck. We're trying to locate his next of kin."

"How is he?" He leapt from the recliner and vaulted to the bedroom to tug on fresh jeans and a T-shirt.

"He's at Texas Presbyterian in Denton. I'm afraid it doesn't look good, sir."

Think. What was Hank's dad's name? "His family lives in Denton. I know his dad's name, but I'm drawing a blank."

"No wife or girlfriend?"

"They're separated. I don't know where she is." Hank's wife left him six months ago. He'd promised to clean up his act and win her back. But now, he might never get the chance.

"Do you know anyone we can contact to get us in touch with his family?"

Phillip. The name came out of nowhere. "His dad's name is Phillip Andrews in Denton."

"Thank you, sir. I appreciate your help, and I'm real sorry about your employee."

"Friend. He's my friend." A sinking lodged in his gut. Hank was gone or would be soon. He could hear the unspoken words in the officer's tone.

The line went dead.

Hank's family would show up, frantic and looking to him for answers. He'd let Hank down. He should have encouraged him to go into a treatment center. If he'd been a better accountability partner, Hank would still be alive.

Quinn glanced at the clock, 11:23 p.m. It was late, but he needed a friend. Clay? No. They didn't really know each other well. Lacie? She'd be there for him, no matter what. And only Lacie could comfort his soul. He scanned through his cell contacts and punched in the number.

Two rings.

"Hello?" Lacie's voice, thick with sleep.

"It's Quinn. I'm real sorry to call so late, but Hank—my friend—he's been in a car accident. I don't think he's gonna pull through and I—" Can't do this alone. But he shouldn't be bothering her with this.

"Hang tight. I'll be right over."

Tense, worried people swarmed the waiting room.

Lacie blew out a big sigh and glanced at Quinn.

He stared at the floor, eyes bloodshot and swollen. "Where'd you say Max is?"

"With Clay and Rayna."

"Oh yeah." He nodded. "The drive over was a blur."

"Good thing I drove."

Hank's family had settled down from teary outbursts to quiet sniffles as the hours ticked past.

"More than likely, he was drinking and driving," Quinn

whispered. "I guess we can be thankful he didn't kill anyone. But I'm having a hard time being thankful about anything. I failed him."

"No. You didn't. You tried to help him."

"I should've gotten him in a treatment center."

"That was a decision he had to make." Her hand rested on his shoulder. "You couldn't make it for him. And I'm betting you tried to convince him."

"I should've tried harder."

"You can't blame yourself."

A doctor entered the room, his expression tense. "Andrews family?"

Hank's dad stood.

"I'm sorry, sir." The doctor shook his head. "We did everything we could."

Hank's mom slumped into her chair.

Quinn's eyes closed. He faced the wall, leaning his forehead against it.

She couldn't let him blame himself. The least she could do was provide comfort. Lacie lay a tentative hand on his back.

He turned, and their eyes locked.

A soul-deep groan escaped him. He engulfed her in his arms. No more sound came, but his shoulders shook for a long time.

Quinn sank into his couch, covering his face with both hands. He'd never been so bone-tired in his whole life. "Why, Lord? Why? Hank was young. He had his whole life ahead of him."

He hadn't called out to God in over two years. And He'd questioned God's judgment then, too. Why had Mel died? Why had Hank died? Why did good men die young? Leaving him guilty in both cases.

He tugged his boots off and lay back.

Lacie had stayed with him until the Andrews family left

and had driven him home. And she'd invited him to church in
the morning. The same church Clay had invited him to ever
since he moved to Aubrey.

He hadn't been to church since Mel died. He wasn't worthy to enter a church. Everywhere he went, people seemed
to die, leaving the blame at his feet.

He'd actually thought if he could help Hank, it might ab-
solve his guilt over Mel's death. But he'd failed Hank.

"I can't do this alone anymore, God. I know I'm not worthy, but I need help."

None are worthy, My son.

Quinn jumped up and scanned the room. No one here but
him. The television and radio remained off. But he'd heard
the voice. God's voice?

He grabbed his cell and jabbed in the number.

"Warren Dude Ranch. Your vacation destination," Clay
drawled.

"It's Quinn."

"Sorry about your friend. Lacie told us what happened.
Need me to come over?"

"No, I'm going to bed. But I wanted to make sure she got
back all right. She wouldn't let me drive her. And—I was
wondering what time church starts in the morning."

"Ten for Sunday school and eleven for service. Want us to
come get you, so you don't have to walk in alone?"

"No, I'll probably just make it for service. See you then."
He closed the phone.

A dusty Bible lay on the shelf under the coffee table. Quinn
picked it up for the first time since that fateful rodeo. The
rustle of the pages comforted his soul as he flipped to the
Twenty-third Psalm.

Lacie settled Max on her lap and stifled a yawn.

How was Quinn this morning? Had he slept any more
than she had?

"Big boy." Max scrambled onto the pew seat beside her.

Lately, he'd insisted he was a big boy a lot. She didn't like this new phase. But she had to let him grow and stretch. Even though she'd like him to be, he couldn't be her baby forever.

Kendra, Rayna, and Gabby would be along soon. The church had welcomed Lacie with open arms. It was growing on her, and since Mel had never attended this church with her, she didn't miss him quite as badly here.

"Mr. Quinn!" Max twisted around in his pew and stood up, arms stretched out.

"My mama always taught me it's rude to turn around and gawk at people as they come in the church. We have to sit still and be quiet." She scooped him up and sat him down, facing forward. "And I'm certain it's not Mr. Quinn. He doesn't go to church."

"Until today." Quinn's voice came from the end of her pew.

Her jaw dropped. "What are you doing here—I mean I'm glad you came."

Max clambered to him.

Quinn held him close and settled beside her.

A male hand squeezed Quinn's shoulder from behind them. "Anything I can do for you?"

"I'm fine. Thanks, Clay."

"Cway." Max reached for Clay.

"Come here, wrangler." Clay scooped up the toddler. "Oh, Lacie, I almost forgot—Brother Timothy's looking for volunteers to work the church booth at the Peanut Festival. Can we put you down?"

"Sure."

"When is it?" Quinn asked.

"First Saturday in October."

"I can help if you need me to. I mean, I'm new here at church, but I plan on sticking around."

"Great, I'll put you down." Clay lifted Max to his shoul-

ders. "I'll deliver this little wrangler to the nursery for you, Lace."

"Thanks." Her heart did a happy dance. Quinn in church. And he planned on sticking around there. "I am glad you came."

"Me, too. I've been carrying a lot of burdens on my own. Feeling unworthy to darken the doors of a church. But Hank's death the other night drove me to my knees. I finally figured out none of us are worthy, but He takes us on anyway."

The main thing that had held her back from getting too close to him. And God had taken care of it. If only it hadn't taken poor Hank's death to get him back in contact with God.

"When's the funeral?"

"Tuesday at a church over in Denton. Afternoon service. Think they're trying to locate his wife. I was hoping—"

"Want me to come with you?"

"I do. But I hate taking you away from Max."

"Max naps in the afternoons."

"I'd appreciate it."

The pianist began playing.

It had been over two years. She was lonely. She'd known Quinn since she was eighteen, and he was a good man. He was great with Max. And now he was back in fellowship with God.

He was the only man who'd made her feel anything since Mel died. Would Mel want her to move forward?

The haunting, tugging strains of "Just as I Am" filled the sanctuary. Lacie blinked. She'd daydreamed through the song service and sermon, all the way to the altar call.

As the congregation sang, Quinn went forward.

Lacie bowed her head. *Lord, help me to do the right thing.* The music faded. Lacie ended her prayer.

Brother Timothy and Quinn stood facing the congregation. "This is Quinn Remington. He recommitted his life to Christ this morning and would like to join our church."

Amens and applause echoed through the church.

Her heart ricocheted.

Please give me peace, with or without Quinn in my life.

The funeral had been wrenching. Hank's distraught mother sobbed through the whole thing, and Quinn wanted to, too.

If only he'd been a better Christian. He could have witnessed to Hank. Where was Hank spending eternity? Quinn didn't know. That lack of knowledge twisted his gut.

At least the steel-gray box in front of the pulpit stayed closed throughout the service. Seeing Hank's pale, lifeless face at the hospital, and the endless hours of visitation last night, had been far more than enough.

He aimed Lacie toward the exit and stayed close on her heels. Escape was ten feet away. Out the church's lobby door.

"Quinn?" a male voice said over his left shoulder.

Hank's dad.

"We really appreciate you for trying to help Hank. Most folks would have fired him."

If I had, he wouldn't have had the money to get drunk and get himself killed.

Lacie's fingers wove through his.

"I'm to blame for his drinking." Hank's father's eyes filled with unshed tears. "I quit a few years ago, but it was too late for Hank. He learned his way of life from me. But he really was trying, and he gave you a lot of the credit for his sober days."

"Me?"

"He told us your faith in him gave him strength and made him respect himself."

Quinn swallowed hard. "Thank you for telling me. You know, you didn't make Hank drink."

Lacie squeezed his hand.

"No, but he learned how by watching me."

"We can't blame ourselves. In the end, we have to realize Hank made his own decisions."

Hank's distraught father nodded and hurried back to his wife's side.

Quinn bolted for the exit, helped Lacie in his truck, and started the engine.

"Was Hank's wife there?"

"No. Reckon when she said she was done, she meant it."

"Quinn?"

Her beauty stalled his breath. Something had changed between them since he recommitted to Christ. Something palpable and alive vibrated between them.

She touched his shoulder, sending quakes through his soul. "You helped Hank. Even though things didn't turn out like we'd like, you gave him respect, and he wanted to do better because of your encouragement."

Her words comforted like a soothing balm, but her nearness stirred things he had no right to long for.

"It takes a strong man to make the right decision when life gets tough. You recommitted to Christ, and I'm proud of you for how you've handled everything the world's thrown at you lately."

"Proud enough to have dinner with me?"

Silence.

"We've had dinner together as a rescue effort"—he tried to keep his voice casual—"and with friends. Don't you think it's time we had dinner alone, just because we want to?"

"You mean like a date?" Her voice quivered.

"Yes." *Our first and last.*

"It's been so long since I… Can I think about it?"

"Sure." He tried to keep the disappointment out of his voice. "No pressure."

What was he thinking? He had no right to ask her. He'd had a long talk with Jesus last night, and his guilt over Mel's

death had ebbed. But he still had no right to romance Mel's widow. Not until he told her the truth. And after that, he might never see her again.

Quinn eased the roof of the white canopy tent up as high as it would go. October lowered the temperature to the upper seventies. Today was a gift. A nice sunny day spent with Lacie at the Peanut Festival.

At the opposite leg of the tent, Lacie reached above her head and couldn't raise the catch as high as it needed to be. But he knew she liked doing things on her own.

She glanced his way. "You okay?"

"I had to interview prospective ranch hands to replace Hank this week."

"I'm sorry. But haven't you heard? Life goes on." She sighed. "I can't begin to tell you how many times I've heard that. I decided the next well-meaning friend who said it to me was gonna get socked in the nose. But I knew they meant well."

Even without her knowing the truth, Mel's ghost stood between them.

With his side of the roof locked in place, she still struggled with hers. Surely, she wouldn't mind if he helped at this point. He started across the open area. Her hand slipped and the tent collapsed over them.

"*Oops.*" Melodic giggling led him in the right direction.

"I've got it." He found her and followed her arm up the pole to the catch. The tent's roof lifted off them, and she faced him. Bright-eyed and beautiful. Boy how he'd love to kiss her. Right here in front of half of Aubrey. Numerous other tents were in set-up progress across the open field, but maybe no one watched them.

No pressure. His own words haunted him.

He backed away and concentrated on the catch on the other two legs. With everything sturdy, he moved two tables under

the canopy while Lacie set out peanut butter balls, brittle, and turtles. Jars of homemade peanut butter lined up alongside cellophane bags of trail mix. Even with all the goodies surrounding them, he could barely keep his eyes off her.

Focus on something besides her. "I understand Aubrey used to be famous for growing peanuts."

"True. The sandy soil was great for growing them." She pointed to a tall, metal, leaning-tower contraption in the back of the field. "That's the peanut dryer. The festival started in 1986 when peanuts were still the main crop around here."

"Do folks still grow peanuts in these parts?"

"No." She waved away a fly, though cellophane covered the food. "Somehow the climate changed. By the time Mel and I moved here, they didn't grow like they used to. But the sandy soil is perfect for horses."

"And Aubrey became Horse Country USA."

"Which is what drew you here."

Not really. But he couldn't tell her that. "Maybe we could have lunch at Moms when our relief crew shows up."

"Maybe."

"No pressure. Not a date. Just two volunteers sharing lunch. I've been craving another Philly Beef & Cheese ever since last Sunday."

"Yum. Okay, I'm in. And by the way, is your offer still open for dinner sometime?"

Does a horse eat hay? "Anytime."

"I'd like that."

His heart sped. "I'm announcing at Cowtown tonight. But I'm off next Saturday night. There's a great Italian place over in Denton."

"I love Italian."

If only she could love him. But she couldn't, not after he told her the truth.

Lacie plopped on the end of her bed. In a mere four days, she'd go to dinner with Quinn. A date. Now was the time.

Max and Danielle had just gone down for their nap. Kendra probably wouldn't be back to retrieve her daughter for a while.

She twisted her wedding rings round and round, inching them toward her knuckle. Finally, they slid off her finger. She sucked in a deep breath, lips trembling.

"I'm so sorry, Mel. If I had my way, you'd still be here. But you're not. I have to live again. Without you."

Her hand trembled as she set the rings on her dresser, and then she lay across her bed. Shaky fingers traced the pale indention they'd left. Her breath came in short bursts.

Chapter 9

"Is this right, Lord?" Lacie whispered.

Her nerves settled. Peace flowed through her.

"Knock, knock," Kendra called.

Lacie hurried to the door.

"Are the munchkins asleep?"

"They are. I didn't expect you back so soon. You could've shopped for another thirty minutes before they're up from their nap."

Kendra's shoulders slumped. "I wasn't shopping. I went to see our lawyer about Danielle's adoption."

"And?" Lacie gestured to the navy couch. The suite was dark and masculine from when Clay had lived there. Temporary. She needed to do something permanent soon.

Closing her eyes, Kendra sank into the cushions. "He says we're safe."

"That's great news! So why aren't you happy?"

"Because I've seen the news—toddlers ripped away from

the only parents they've ever known at the whim of some judge."

Lacie squeezed Kendra's hand. "I think that's very rare. And you don't know Lynn wants her back. They're moving home; that's all."

Kendra scanned Lacie's hand. "Your rings?"

Pinpricks bloomed at the back of Lacie's eyes. She blinked. "I'm going to dinner with Quinn Saturday night. I didn't think I should wear my wedding rings on a—"

"A date. How do you feel?"

Her vision blurred. *Like I'm turning my back on Mel and all we shared.* "Torn. But I'm so tired of being alone. I've known Quinn for a long time, and I always liked him. But lately—"

"You're attracted to him." Kendra elbowed her. "That's good, honey. You're still alive, and you need to live. Mel wouldn't want you to spend your life mourning him."

Lacie nodded. "Quinn's a good man."

"He's even been coming to church."

"That was the final hurdle holding me back."

"Now it's full steam ahead, for both of us." Kendra swiped her eyes and propped her feet on the cedar coffee table. "We both need to get out of our funks."

"Stop borrowing trouble." Lacie grinned. "I'll pray for you, and you pray for me."

"Done."

"What if he wants to kiss me?" Lacie pressed trembling fingers to her lips. "Mel was the only man I've ever kissed."

"You'll remember how. Or tell him you're not ready. Don't let him rush you—into anything. But then, I don't think Quinn's that kind of guy. Just go to dinner, have a nice time, and enjoy the company of a nice Christian man."

That was her problem—she already enjoyed his company, way too much.

She'd never been the type to date just for the fun of it. Es-

pecially now, with Max. But was she ready for something lasting? Was Quinn?

Lacie covered her face with both hands. "I don't even know if I really feel anything for him. Or if I'm just lonely and he's familiar."

"You'll never know unless you stick your big toe in the water." Kendra patted her shoulder. "Have you prayed about Quinn?"

"Yes."

"And?"

"Perfect peace."

"Well, there you go. God's got it covered. Just follow His lead."

Into the arms of another man? How, when part of her heart still belonged to Mel?

Tennis shoes squeaked on the laminate flooring as Lacie stopped in front of the fireplace. The longest week of her life. Only Thursday. Would Saturday ever come?

"What do you think of the house?" Mama asked.

Lacie snapped to attention. "It's nice. Very homey and cozy."

"That's what I thought. Star's a great real estate agent."

Star tapped her chin with a perfectly manicured fingernail. "You need a big rug for in here. Center the living room furniture around it. Fireplaces are so romantic."

Lacie smoothed her hand over the marble hearth.

Mama gasped. "Lacie?"

She jerked away, like a kid caught with her hand in the cookie jar. "What? Does it scratch easy?"

"Your rings."

Warmth coursed through her body, creeping up her neck, and boiling her cheeks. "I'll tell you if you won't push."

"I promise." Mama shot her a Girl Scout salute.

"Me, too." Star crossed her heart.

"I'm going to dinner with Quinn."

Mama's hands jerked together as if to clap then stopped. "That's wonderful, dear. I hope you enjoy yourself." She swept her hand toward the wall. "I thought we'd put your grandfather's bookcase over here. But what on earth will I put over the fireplace? We don't have any artwork big enough."

Who'd have guessed Mama was capable of such self-control?

"I love you." Lacie hugged her mom. "Let's go shopping before the move. We should be able to find something perfect at the Galleria."

"*Ooh*, sounds fun. We could invite your father, too. He could hang out at the man stores and meet us for lunch. Maybe Quinn could go with him, only to keep him from getting bored, of course."

Lacie rolled her eyes. She'd known it was too good to last.

"I love you, too, dear."

"I know." Lacie grinned.

"You have to admit Mama's holding herself back quite admirably." Star propped her chin on her fist. "I wonder if Wyatt would want to go?"

Lacie's jaw dropped. "Wyatt?"

A blush pinked Star's cheeks. "He looked me up in the phone book after you introduced us at the rodeo. We've talked on the phone a few times, but I get the feeling he has some baggage. I've been meaning to ask you about him."

"You know this guy, Lacie?" Mama's protector mode shifted into overdrive.

"He's a bull rider." Lacie tucked her hands in her pockets. "A year ago, I'd have said, 'Run the other way.' He was the all-time womanizer and a big jerk. But his girlfriend got pregnant, and she wanted to abort. That forced him to his knees."

"He told me he got saved, and he's raising his baby girl alone." Star shook her head. "That must be tough."

"It is, but he's crazy about her. He talked his ex into car-

rying the baby to term, and she signed all rights over to him. He's like a different person. Completely focused on Jesus and his daughter."

"Sounds like a keeper to me." Mama's eyes narrowed, the way they did when she hatched a plan. "I assume Wyatt and Quinn know each other. All the more reason to invite Quinn on our outing."

The invitation would definitely show the men's true colors. What guy wanted to spend the day with the girl he wanted to date—and her parents?

"Just know that if you date Wyatt, Hannah is part of the package."

"I love kids. Especially girls."

Lacie could imagine Hannah, usually dressed in baby-cowgirl gear or overalls, after Star played dress-up with her.

"Does Quinn realize you're a package deal?" Mama asked.

"Yes, but it's one date, Mama. Not a lifetime commitment." Mama didn't need to know it was anything more than casual. And she didn't plan to include Max in the package just yet.

Quinn stared at Giuseppe's menu, though he knew he'd order the same thing he always did. The two-story Victorian house with warm rust-colored walls usually relaxed him. But not tonight. Not with Lacie sitting across from him.

"Yum, I think I'll have this pasta-thingy I can't pronounce, with grilled shrimp."

"Capellini Rustico." The server said it with an authentic-sounding accent, saving Quinn from butchering the name for her. "And for you, sir?"

"I'll go with the lasagna." He could pronounce it, and he'd never met a lasagna he didn't love.

"Excellent choice." The server took the menus and hurried away.

Lacie looked up at him. The future shone bright in her eyes.

But could they scale the all-time relationship roadblock? He had to tell her.

Had any man ever killed a man and ended up with his widow? King David had, but it hadn't gone so well for him.

Just as well it ended now, before his heart got any more attached to her.

"Did you find a new ranch hand?"

"Not yet."

Her hand covered his.

His heart danced a jig. But he couldn't allow it to.

"I have to tell you something." Their voices blended together.

She giggled. "You first."

If he told her, he'd never see that smile or hear her laugh again.

He had to tell her, but couldn't he at least enjoy her company first? "You go ahead."

"This is the first date I've been on since I can't remember when, and I'm terrified."

And it would be their last. "Nothing to be afraid of."

"I have to confess: I'm very attracted to you." She blushed.

Quinn's heart sank.

"Maybe I'm saying too much, but I need to let you know where things stand. I've been fighting my feelings for you for a while. Your walk with Christ held me back, but when you went to the altar, you took away my major qualm about you." She squeezed his hand.

He covered it with his. Something wasn't right. He glanced down. Rings gone. His gaze caught hers and held.

He couldn't crush her. Not now, when she was trying to move on. With him.

"What did you need to tell me?"

"I've had a crush on you since high school."

She laughed again. A lyrical sound.

"Did you know?"

"No. But Mama did. She never said anything then, but she's been trying to convince me since we reconnected."

"Mamas are always right." His fingers threaded through hers. "So your major qualm about me is gone. Got any others?"

Her eyes closed, and moisture seeped from under her lashes. "Mel. I feel like I'm betraying him."

Me, too.

"I'm sorry. Here I am, bawling on our first date." She dabbed her eyes with her napkin. "Maybe I'm not ready. I just don't know."

"We can take things as slowly as you need to. I won't even try to kiss you good night. Not until you let me know you're ready."

Her posture relaxed as if a huge weight slipped off her shoulders.

"Tell me about Mel."

She frowned. "Our first date and you want to talk about my husband?"

Maybe talking about him could help remove the ghost standing between them. "If you're okay with it."

"We met at a rodeo in the summer between my junior and senior years." She shrugged. "He'd already graduated and was traveling the circuit, and I was Miss Rodeo Texas Teen. It was love at first sight." Her expression turned dreamy.

Quinn tried not to squirm, waiting until she came back from wherever her mind had taken her.

"I went to his rodeos as much as I could during my senior year, and he came to my events as often as he could. Our long-distance romance got old quick, and Mel asked me to marry him." Her fingers traced the pale indention where her rings had been. "I wanted to quit school and get married, but Daddy wouldn't let me. Besides, I had to fulfill my Miss Rodeo Texas Teen obligations. So as soon as I graduated and passed on my crown, we got married."

"And set up house in Aubrey."

"I traveled to all his rodeos with him. Mel wanted me to keep barrel racing, but we were on the road so much, I didn't get enough practice, and it fell by the wayside." She nibbled her lip. "But I really didn't miss it. I was too much in love and couldn't focus on anything other than praying him through every bull ride.

"After a few years we settled down, and Mel pretty much rode only at the Stockyards, but then he did well, and we had to start traveling to Horizon rodeos and then the Cinch rodeos." Her words tumbled out as if she hadn't had anyone to talk with about Mel in a while. "But, I was tired of the road and...found out I was pregnant with Max. Did you know Mel was planning to retire the season he died?"

Quinn swallowed the lump in his throat. "I think I read something about it."

"All those years, I was so careful not to get pregnant in case something happened to him." She pressed her fist to her temple. "I know God's in control. But sometimes, I wonder why, when we were about to have a baby, Mel had to die."

At my hands. "I reckon we'll understand God's timing when we get to heaven someday."

"And live in the meantime." She wiped her eyes again. "Without questioning. Without looking back."

"Moving forward. Together."

Her laugh came out soggy. "I won't hold my breath for you to call me again."

"Why wouldn't I?" Why did Mel's widow have to be the woman he'd loved since high school?

"Because I spent half our date blubbering over my husband."

"You don't blubber. You cry pretty, and I'd rather be your shoulder to lean on than have some other guy fit the bill."

He still had to tell her. But not now. Let their relationship develop. Then maybe she'd be able to forgive him. Or not.

If not—his heart would never recover.

At least he'd have this time he'd spent with her to console himself with.

Selfish love-struck coward. That's what he was.

Lacie hurried to the sanctuary after dropping Max in the nursery. He'd fussed this morning, and she hated disrupting services by being late. Rayna wasn't in the nursery this week, but if she gave into Max's fussing, she'd never get him used to his new church family.

A teenage boy almost ran into her and then ducked his head, but not fast enough to hide his black eye. He rushed down the empty hall.

He looked familiar. Come on, think. Trent. Danielle's father. Stetson and Kendra's Danielle. Only, he didn't know, or did he?

"Trent?"

He stopped but didn't turn to face her.

"Honey, what happened?"

Silence.

"Do you need to talk to the youth director or the pastor?"

"I was hoping to talk to Stetson."

"Church has already started, but I can go get him. Did someone hit you?"

His shoulders slumped. "My dad."

"Oh honey." She touched his arm.

Trent jerked away.

"I want to help you. I'm a friend of Stetson's."

He faced her, fury etched in his tense features.

He was bigger than her, and they were alone in a deserted hall.

Chapter 10

Inwardly, Lacie cringed. Don't show fear. Don't let him see you sweat. If she screamed, would they hear her in the sanctuary?

"He kicked me out." Trent's voice broke, despite his rage.

"Why?" Relax. *He's not angry with me.* Just a boy, hurt by the man he should be able to trust.

"He was drunk, and I wanted to go to church." Trent raked his hand through his hair. "I couldn't find the truck keys, so I woke him up to ask where they were. Guess it made him mad."

Lacie shuddered. "What about your mom?"

"She left us." Trent's voice hardened. "A long time ago."

So not equipped for this. In her world, families loved each other and stayed together.

"You go in the youth room." She patted his arm. "I'll go get Stetson. And we'll find you a place to stay."

Trent nodded and trudged to the youth room.

She ran down the hall. Her mother's words echoed from

childhood—no running in the church. But with her heart in her throat, her feet didn't slow.

What was up with Lacie? About the time Quinn decided she was skipping church, she entered the sanctuary and whispered something to Stetson. He left and still hadn't returned. Beside Quinn, but eons away, tension rolled off Lacie through the sermon. He ached to put his arm around her. She practically ran to the altar as soon as the closing hymn began.

Teary eyed, she came back and stood beside him.

The altar call closed, and a deacon dismissed them with prayer. The crowd began to disperse.

"Are you okay?" Quinn whispered.

"It's one of the boys from the youth group." Lacie's voice caught. "His dad hit him and kicked him out."

Quinn shook his head. "What would possess a man to do such a thing?"

"Alcohol."

"How old is this boy?"

"I think he's eighteen."

"Wonder if he's ever done any ranch work?"

One corner of her mouth lifted. "You still need a hand? I don't know if he has any experience."

"I could train him."

"That would be awesome. Now he just needs a place to stay."

"I can take care of that, too. Hank lived in a cabin on my property."

She grabbed his arm. "You'd really do that?"

"Sure, why not?"

"You don't even know him."

"No, but he needs help, and I'm in a position to help."

She hugged him.

Right there in church.

He could get used to it.

* * *

An elbow jabbed Lacie in the ribs as she stepped inside Moms. She adjusted Max on her hip and turned around.

"I take it things went well on your date?" Kendra whispered. "Y'all were awful cozy in church this morning. I saw that hug."

Lacie smiled, and warmth spread through her. "Good. Really good."

"I'm so glad. Did he ask you out again?"

"We're having dinner before the rodeo Friday night."

"Are you still torn?"

"Not as bad." The character she'd seen him show this morning—helping a boy he didn't even know—made her like him even more. "Did you hear about what's going on with Trent?"

"Stetson told me about his dad. The jerk."

"Quinn's gonna let him stay at his ranch and hire him as a hand."

Kendra blew out a deep breath. "Oh, I'm so relieved. I mean, Trent's really come a long way, and I'd love to help him, but I was so afraid Stetson would invite him to live with us. And since Danielle… Oh, I'm a terrible youth director's wife."

"No." Lacie squeezed her arm. "You're a loving, concerned mom."

"Where is Trent now? Is he coming to lunch with us?"

"Brother Timothy wanted to talk to him. Quinn's supposed to pick him up after lunch."

"Want us to give y'all some space?"

"No, we'll sit with our friends."

"There you are." Quinn reached toward Max. "Let me have this little guy. Ready to order?"

Max shifted to Quinn, his little arms reaching out.

A chasm roiled in her stomach; Lacie handed him over. "Starving."

They placed their orders and hurried to the party room

next door. A new antique pay phone graced the wall near their usual large table. Soon Rayna and Clay joined them. Quinn claimed the seat beside Lacie, and Stetson blessed the food.

"Christmas on Main's coming up soon." Clay scanned the faces at the table. "I'm signing up volunteers for the church's booth. It's the Saturday before Thanksgiving from ten to three. Any takers?"

Quinn wiped mashed potatoes from Max's cheek. "Another festival?"

"The owners of Moms handle it. And again, the proceeds go to the library."

"I'm sure Lacie and I can help." Quinn said it as if they were a couple. Couldn't get one without the other.

Her face warmed, but it was a happy blush.

Quinn had the definite feeling he and Wyatt were being tested. Especially when the women went shopping, leaving Wyatt and him with Lacie's dad, Gerald. Quinn still couldn't get used to calling him that.

They browsed through the Dallas Cowboys Pro Shop, Finish Line, and Champs, then agreed none of them were big shoppers and found a bench in the middle of the mall.

Gerald grilled them both about their lives, their ambitions, and laid down the law on how his daughters were to be treated. Then the conversation relaxed.

They discussed everything from the Maxwells' upcoming move to livestock, politics, and church. At least there weren't any uncomfortable silences, and they agreed on most topics.

Quinn's heart sped when he saw the women heading in their direction. One woman in particular. Lacie, a puff of white in her coat with a fur collar and cuffs. Beautiful with a light shining in her eyes. Because of him?

"Hungry yet?" Her mom—Karen—carried numerous shopping bags.

"Starving." All three men chorused.

"But by the looks of things, we may not have enough left in our account to eat on." Gerald's arm slung over Quinn's shoulders. "You buying?"

"Sure."

Karen slapped Gerald's arm. "I just bought a few things for the house, and most of it was on sale."

"Uh huh. What's on the menu?"

"Sbarro's." Lacie's voice blended with her sister.

"The girls' favorite. You guys okay with Italian?"

"My favorite." His words mixed with Wyatt's.

It really was Quinn's favorite. Was Wyatt just trying to impress?

Quinn fit right in with Lacie's family. They were so warm, and they'd taken Wyatt right in, too.

The future looked bright. Married to Lacie, raising Max, part of this family. Did her thoughts lead in that direction? He hoped so. He prayed so. But could their future together handle the truth? Who was he kidding? Their future should be based on the truth.

Ice skaters sailed around the rink, located in the middle of the food court. Burgers, onions, and garlic filled his senses. His stomach rumbled as they rode the escalator up to the third level.

Lacie stared down at the skaters.

"Do you skate?"

"I always wanted to. You?"

"I played hockey."

"You know, I'd forgotten that. I was always off to horse shows, and you played hockey."

"Wanna skate after we eat?"

"Oh no, I couldn't. I'd fall flat on my face."

"No, you wouldn't." He held his hand out to her. "I'd be there to catch you."

She blushed and slipped her fingers into his. "Okay. Sounds like fun."

* * *

Lacie held Quinn's hands in a death grip. Effortlessly, he skated backward and pulled her along.

"Relax."

"I can't. Every time I try, my feet slide everywhere."

"I've got you. Relax. Think about something else."

"How's Trent doing?"

"Great. He's a hard worker. Helping him's like getting another chance with Hank."

"You're a good man, Quinn."

His mouth twitched, and something died in his eyes. "You're still not relaxed. You feel like a statue."

She took a deep breath, and her feet slid in opposite directions, dangerously close to achieving the split she'd never been able to master in cheerleading.

Quinn's hands gripped her waist and lifted her slightly.

"I won't let you fall, Lacie. Ever."

Dangerously close to him, but her feet were under her again, gliding with his. Yet her feet were the last thing on her mind. His aftershave filled her senses. Rich and spicy. His green eyes locked with hers.

He stopped in front of her.

Lacie slammed into Quinn. She yelped.

His arms came around her, steadying her.

Strength. Warmth. And all male. She hadn't been this close to a man since—

"Might want to watch where you're going," Wyatt's voice said behind Quinn, and then he skated into view, holding Star's hands.

"Sorry, y'all okay?" Quinn swiveled toward them, his arms still around Lacie.

"Fine." Star glided effortlessly by with Wyatt, her smile huge. "Isn't he a great skater?"

"I played hockey." Wyatt's voice was gruff. "A real man's sport. Otherwise, I'd have never done this kind of thing."

"Don't worry, Wyatt, you're the macho man," Lacie's tone teased. "Even on ice skates."

Wyatt growled, and he and Star sailed away.

"Looks like they're getting along good." Quinn looked down at her. "You okay?"

She nodded, unable to find her voice.

He pulled away, clasping her hands once more. "How come Star can skate and you can't?"

Minus his warmth, a chill crept through her. "Star decided to teach me once, so she took me to the top of our grandmother's steep driveway and pushed me down. Needless to say, I rolled the whole way and I never would try again."

"Siblings are great for stuff like that. I was always kind of glad I didn't have any." Quinn glanced behind him. "I think your folks might be ready to leave."

He skated her over to the rail where her parents stood.

She felt like a mannequin, stiff and afraid to even try to move her feet.

"Why don't y'all join us?" Quinn asked.

"I would if it wasn't for my bad knee." Daddy scooped up their pile of shopping bags. "Old football injury."

"We're calling it a day." Mama shot Lacie a knowing smile. "You kids stay and have fun. I'm sure Quinn and Wyatt can get y'all home."

"Safe and sound." Quinn let go of one of her hands to shake Daddy's. "Thanks for including me today. I really enjoyed it."

Daddy clapped him on the back. Like he used to Mel. As if Quinn were part of their family.

Replacing Mel.

Lacie pulled loose from Quinn, clamped both hands on the railing, and then pulled herself along it to the exit. "I'm ready to go now, anyway. Wyatt can bring Star home, but I'll ride with Mama and Daddy."

He caught up with her and whispered, "I thought we were having fun."

"We were. But I need to get home and pick up Max. He'll be up from his nap by now, and I don't want to take advantage of Clay's mom since she won't let me pay her."

"Are we still on Friday night?"

She should cancel. Though everything inside her said flee, she longed to be with him. "Sure."

His features relaxed.

The tidal wave building inside her didn't.

Quinn squeezed Lacie's hand as they left Cattlemen's Steakhouse. She'd been quiet during dinner.

He huddled her in the crook of his arm, waiting for the light to change. Hand in hand, they crossed the brick-lined street and walked toward the Coliseum.

"I've always wanted to try the maze. It's a warm day. Want to give it a whirl?" he asked.

Her face froze.

Was she claustrophobic or something?

"It's not a big deal." He checked his watch. "We've got some time before the rodeo, and I've heard a lot about it, but it's okay if you don't want to."

"No, it's always fun. Let's go." But tension careened off her in waves.

Quinn's eyes squeezed shut. "You did the maze with Mel, didn't you?"

"Lots of times." She smiled, lost in a memory. "We nearly got thrown out once 'cause Mel kissed me. A worker saw us from the observation tower. We told him we were married, and he let us off with the promise of no more PDAs."

Pink crept up her neck. "Sorry. I don't know why I told you that."

"Because, it was a good memory. I don't mind if you talk about Mel. He was part of your life long before I was."

She relaxed. Her hand squeezed his. "Maybe we could make some new memories."

"But"—he wagged a finger at her—"no PDAs."

Lacie giggled and pulled him toward the maze.

The maze worker stamped the time on two cards imprinted with the word *Maze*.

"There's four punch machines, one with each letter in the maze," Lacie explained. "You have to find each one and then find the exit."

Holding hands, they entered the human-size maze, based on the old Stockyards cattle pens.

Quinn grinned. Rubber rats were nailed to the overhead rafters. After a few turns, he felt like a big rat.

Are You Lost?—asked a big yellow sign.

He was definitely lost. In more ways than one. Having Lacie so close did a number on his heart. Think about something else, other than how good her hand feels. Something else besides how much he wanted to steal a kiss from her.

"Have you ever brought Max here?"

She laughed. "Are you kidding? Little booger would shimmy right under and get away."

Probably eighteen inches clearance at the bottom of the maze. "You wouldn't have any trouble going after him. Besides, I'd hang onto him. Let's bring him sometime."

She stiffened. Her grip on his hand went cold. "No."

"Did I say something wrong?"

Chapter 11

"I don't want Max getting attached to you in case—" Lacie's voice came out too tight.

Quinn's smile died. "In case things don't work out between us?"

"Yes." She couldn't let Max get hurt. No matter how she felt about Quinn.

He stopped and settled his hands on her shoulders. "I'm not going anywhere. Are you?"

"You just never know about relationships." Her gaze flitted away from his. "I don't want Max getting too used to having you around."

"I see him at church. We take him to lunch afterward." Quinn held both palms upward. "Why would taking him to the maze be any different?"

"Because it would just be us. On a date."

"It'll be hard." He grinned. "But I can assure you I won't try to steal a kiss with your boy around."

"That's not it." She charged around a corner.

But Quinn was faster.

A few turns later, he caught up with her. "Please, Lacie, stop."

She did, but her gaze went up to the observation booth, where the maze worker frowned down at them.

"Do you need help, ma'am?"

"No." Lacie forced a smile.

"We're fine." Quinn waved to the man and lowered his voice for her ears only. "Let's work together and get out of this thing. Then we'll talk."

She gave him a stiff nod. At least he didn't try to hold her hand. The urge to flee boiled inside her, but she stayed with him, and they made their way through the maze.

Punch cards, now an unwanted distraction, she found the entry and vaulted toward it.

"You sure you're okay, ma'am?" The maze worker met them. "Do you feel light-headed or short of breath?"

"Just feeling a little claustrophobic, but nothing to worry about." It wasn't the maze that made her feel closed-in. It was Quinn.

"I'll see to her." Quinn pressed a hand to the small of her back. "Maybe something to drink would help."

Lacie stalked away from him. "I don't want anything to drink. I'm fine."

"Then tell me what's wrong." He gestured to a wooden bench under a gnarled, twisted live oak tree. "Let's sit here."

She plopped on the bench. "I won't be one of those moms with a different boyfriend constantly parading through Max's life."

Quinn's eyes rounded in mock surprise. "You have a boyfriend?"

Tears stung.

"Hey, I'm teasing you." He took her hand in his. "Trying to get a smile out of you."

"My son isn't a teasing matter." She jerked her hand away.

"I taught a kid's Sunday school class in our old church. There was this little seven-year-old boy whose mom never came to church. She always had a new boyfriend, who stayed just long enough for the little guy to get attached."

"You could never be one of those moms. If for some reason beyond my control, this doesn't work out between us, and"—he cleared his throat as if the words were hard to say—"and you date someone else, you'll shield Max. Just like you're doing now."

"But I don't want Max to go through that—not even once." Her voice came out a whisper. "I think I made a mistake. Maybe I'm not ready."

"We're not a mistake. I said I'd never push you. And I meant it. I'm sorry. I'll back off Max until you're more secure in our relationship."

She shook her head and stood. "I'm sorry. But I don't think we should see each other anymore."

Her feet didn't want to go. The urge to hurl herself into his arms almost overwhelmed her. But she had to keep Max's well-being first. Not the erratic beat of her heart or the Cowtown Coliseum–sized lump in her throat.

No turning back. Walking away from Quinn was one of the hardest things she'd ever do. But she had to.

Quinn wanted to fall on his knees and beg her to stay in his life. But if he pushed her, she'd only run farther away. She was scared. And he'd pressured her. The thing he'd promised never to do. He hadn't meant to, but he had.

"Can I at least give you a ride home after the rodeo? No strings."

"I'll catch a ride with Kendra." She hurried toward Cowtown Coliseum.

His heart sank as she walked out of his life for good. "Are you still gonna give lessons for me?"

Her footsteps stalled. "Yes, but I'd appreciate it if you made yourself scarce when I'm there."

"Will do." He saluted her back and watched until she disappeared through the doors of the Coliseum. *What do I do now, Lord?*

A rodeo to announce in an hour. Pull it together, pick up his heart from the Trail of Fame where she'd left it.

He stared at the star-shaped, embossed bronze plaque. Annie Oakley. Sharpshooting star of Buffalo Bill's Wild West Show in the late 1800s. A looker, happily married, but probably broke a few hearts in her teen years—fitting for Lacie to shatter his here.

"Quinn." Stetson clapped him on the back. "You going in?"

"Just preparing myself mentally." Forget Lacie.

For now.

Maybe if he kept his distance, she'd miss him. Nice thought. But not much to hang his hat full of hopes on.

What had she been thinking? Obviously, not about Max.

Lacie breathed in the familiar manure of Cowtown Coliseum. She used to feel closer to Mel here. Now Quinn wormed his way into her thoughts.

A rip in the middle of her heart burned in her chest.

Selfish. She'd jumped in with both feet because she was lonely. So what? Her grandmother had been widowed young and left with six kids. She'd kept her farm and raised her family without a man. After her children grew up, she'd met and married Grandpa.

Max had to come first.

Her fingers traced the empty place where her wedding rings should be. Should've never taken them off. Once this endless night ended, they'd go right back on.

"What's wrong?" Kendra settled in the chair beside her. "You're all tense."

Lacie shook her head.

"You and Quinn have a fight?"

"Sort of. I don't know what I was thinking. I'm not ready."
And neither is Max.

"I'd hoped it'd work out between y'all. Maybe Rayna and
I pushed you too much. We want you to be happy."

"I know. And you didn't push me. I'm a big girl." With
big-girl feelings for Quinn. But she had to forget him. Concentrate on raising Max. "I don't know. Maybe I should've
moved to San Antonio. But now, Mama and Daddy have
found a house in Denton."

"Everybody needs family." Kendra patted her knee. "Give
yourself time. You barrel racing tonight?"

Quinn had brought Copper to the Coliseum, but she just
wasn't up for it now. If she rode, would Quinn cheer her on
from the announcer's booth? Or ignore her ride?

"No." She couldn't face it, either way.

The final week of October painted the landscape surrounding Clay's arena in reds and golds. Lacie and Copper charged
around the final barrel and back to the gate. Why was she
practicing her horse if she wasn't going to barrel race?

Quinn had kept his word and made himself scarce during her lessons all week, just as she'd asked him to. But she
missed him.

"Y'all look great," Clay shouted. "But why aren't you over
at Quinn's arena?"

She closed her eyes for a moment then dismounted.

"Trouble in paradise?" A frown pinched Clay's eyebrows.

"He wanted to spend time with Max."

"Horrors." He clamped a hand over his mouth in mock
shock. "I had no idea you were dealing with such a monster."

She stomped her boot. "I'm serious."

"Sorry." Clay climbed the fence and hooked his arms over
the top rail. "Max is part of your package. Most men just

want the woman and ignore their kids. Shouldn't you be glad Quinn cares?"

"I have to protect Max."

"From Quinn."

"From getting too attached."

"So you wanna keep Max away from him until the wedding? Don't you think they need to do some bonding first?"

"There's not going to be any wedding." She socked him in his good shoulder and led Copper to the gate.

Clay opened the gate and fell in stride with her on the way back to the barn. "Listen, I know you miss Mel. And you probably feel like you're betraying him."

Her steps stalled. "He was part of me"—her voice quivered—"for a long time."

"I know. Me, too." He hugged her. "You have to know he'd want you to be happy, to move on."

That's it! She socked him in the shoulder again.

"Hey. What'd I do?"

If anyone could convince her to move on, it was Clay. But she couldn't risk Max getting hurt. He'd already lost so much, before he'd ever been born.

"I told Quinn we can't see each other again." She shook her head. "I'm not ready."

"You ought to know better than anybody."

"You're not going to try to talk me into dating him."

"You're an adult, old enough to make your own call." He gently chucked her chin. "Even if you are a squirt. And besides, my shoulder's getting sore."

She wanted to smile, but she didn't have any left. "Is it okay if I board Copper here again?"

"Only if you promise to still train her for barrels."

She rolled her eyes. "Oh, if you insist. I always feel like I'm tying up your arena."

"You're not." He adjusted his hat. "You still giving lessons over at Quinn's?"

"I can't let my students down. And he promised to stay out of my way." And he had today. She hadn't seen hide nor hair of him. Not that it made her any happier.

"Look, Lace, I want you to be happy." He grabbed her hand, studied her wedding rings on her finger. "And if you're happy being alone, that's fine and dandy with me."

Except—she wasn't happy.

Quinn knocked on the familiar farmhouse door, his feet crunching the dead November leaves that had blown up on the porch. He'd wanted to come home for a while, and the trip got him out of Lacie's way for another week.

He saw movement through the filmy curtains, and the door swung open. Face-to-face with his dad. Gray sprinkled Dad's beard.

How long had it been? Almost three years.

"Son?"

"Hey, Dad."

"Why didn't you tell us you were coming?" Dad pulled him inside and shut the door. He hugged Quinn and roughly clapped him on the back.

Why had he waited so long? The two places he should've turned with his failure—God and his parents. Yet he'd shunned both.

"Quinn." His mother's squeal echoed through the adjoining kitchen. She dashed through the living room and flew into his arms.

Unconditional love surged through her warm embrace. Her Avon Odyssey perfume smelled of flowers and soft musk.

"I can't believe you're here."

"The Maxwells are moving to Denton. I told them I'd planned a trip home anyway, and I offered to help. Came a few days early to visit. Should've called, I guess."

"You're welcome anytime, son. You know that. But if we'd known, your mama could've made a fuss."

Quinn grinned. "Maybe that's why I didn't tell you."

"You shush." Mama pulled away. Her hair was still warm brown. She had the same solid shape, though a bit thicker through the middle, and a few more wrinkles in her face. Her eyes shone too brightly, memorizing his face, as if she thought she wouldn't see him again for a long time.

Yes, he'd definitely stayed away too long.

"A woman's got a right to make a fuss when her only child comes home for a visit. Oh, I don't have a thing to cook." She smacked his shoulder. "If I'd have known you were coming, I'd be prepared. You just got here, and I'll have to go off to the store."

"You've got a freezer full of food, Donna."

"But not Quinn's favorites."

"You don't have to go to any trouble, Mama."

"Nonsense." She patted his cheek. "I'll make a quick run. How long you staying?"

"Through Friday. I'll help get the Maxwells loaded Saturday morning and head out that afternoon."

"Four glorious days with my two favorite guys in the whole world." Mama kissed his cheek. "Don't you go anywhere. I'll be back in two shakes of a rattler's tale."

She grabbed her purse and closed the door behind her.

Daddy sank into his recliner and clicked off the TV. "How far is Aubrey from Denton?"

"'Bout fifteen minutes."

"The Maxwells were always good folk. Wonder why they're moving? How'd you get hooked up with them again?"

"Star's in Denton, and Lacie lives in Aubrey. We're sort of neighbors, and were sort of seeing each other for a while."

"You always had a thing for that girl."

Guilty. The last three weeks of making himself scarce during her lessons and sitting on the far end of their friends' pew had almost killed him.

"But didn't she get married?"

Quinn cleared his throat. "He died." Guilty again.

"Why aren't you 'sort of' seeing her anymore?"

"She's still half in love with her husband, and she's got a little boy she feels like she has to protect."

"Understandable. Why's it been so long since you came home? Sorry for all the questions, but you know your mama will ask when she gets back from the store."

"I messed up, Dad. Big time." Quinn sank onto the couch. "And I didn't talk to anyone about it. Not God. Not y'all. I felt unworthy to be His son or yours. And it's all twisted up with Lacie."

"Lacie? You didn't mess around and get her pregnant, did you, son?"

"I haven't even kissed her, Dad. And she's not like that." But he'd like to marry her, love her fully, raise Max as his own, and maybe have more kids together. But not with this insurmountable secret standing between them.

"I've been holding out on her. Something big. And now I don't know how to tell her. We've two-stepped forward and line danced backward for months. If I tell her the truth, there probably won't be any more dancing." Who was he kidding? His secret was insurmountable even if she knew the truth.

"The truth shall make you free. And those aren't my words, son. Straight from the mouth of Jesus." His father tapped the Bible on the end table. "Tell me about it. Your mama won't be back for a good hour."

Lacie slid the box marked Dishes into the kitchen of her parents' new house. With familiar furnishings, mementos, and family portraits, it would feel like home.

All week, her parents and Clay had made several trips to San Antonio, transporting Clay's stock trailers loaded with their belongings back to Denton. They'd left the big furniture for today. Clay had gathered up help, probably his ranch hands.

Star stared out the kitchen window, her arms crossed over her chest. "I like it. It's newer and nicer than the old place, and it'll be great having Mama and Daddy close. I'll never have to go to San Antonio again and worry about running into my ex and the bimbo he left me for."

"Good riddance." Lacie squeezed Star's arm. "So what about you and Wyatt?"

Star smiled. The kind of down-to-her-toes smile Lacie hadn't seen since Star learned of her ex-husband's affair.

"We get along great. He's fun to be with. And he treats me like a queen. I'm meeting Hannah next week."

"She's a doll. Sounds serious."

"I hope so. What about you and Quinn?"

Lacie shrugged. "I think I jumped the gun. It's no big deal. I need to focus on Max right now."

"Quinn could help you with Max."

"But what if it doesn't work out between us? Then Max would be hurt." Lacie hugged herself.

"I noticed you put your rings back on." Star patted her arm. "Just give yourself time. But I wouldn't keep Quinn stringing along too long. He's a great guy. Some woman will snap him up if you don't."

Had she been stringing him along? She'd redouble her efforts to avoid him. No stringing allowed.

The front door opened, and they scurried to front of the house.

Quinn backed into the living room, carrying one end of her parents' couch.

Her breath stalled.

Daddy held the other end. The men carefully eased it through the door.

"I want it facing the fireplace." Mama called instructions from outside.

While they arranged the sofa, Wyatt wrestled the big-screen TV inside. Star hurried to help him.

Mama followed the men inside. "The couch isn't centered. Move it to the right a smidgen. Right there. Perfect. Now put the TV on the stand over on that side."

"Shouldn't the couch face the TV instead of the fireplace?" Daddy frowned.

"The recliners will face the TV."

"So when we have guests, they'll have to crane their necks to watch TV."

Mama rolled her eyes. "How often do we watch TV when we have guests?"

"Daddy, every stick of furniture can't face the TV." Lacie played mediator. "And besides that, the TV isn't the center of our existence."

"Only during football season." He winked. "Speaking of which, we need to get this show on the road. The game starts at six, and these boys have a rodeo tonight."

Daddy, Mama, Wyatt, and Star headed out the door to unload the trailers.

Quinn followed, but Lacie grabbed his arm. Muscle flexed under her fingertips.

Chapter 12

Lacie jerked her hand away as if she'd been burned. "What are you doing here?"

"I offered to help that day we all went to the mall." Quinn avoided her eyes.

"You're certainly not staying out of my way very well."

"I wouldn't back out on them. And you should be happy I wasn't at the ranch all week during your lessons." He hurried out the door.

She'd probably hurt his feelings. Here he's breaking his back for her parents and she blasted him for it. *It's not all about me.* Deal with Quinn, and be grateful for his help.

If Lacie showed up, the day was cut out to be awkward. Quinn squared his shoulders and cut through the obstacle course of canopy tents that made up Christmas on Main.

Moving her parents into their new house and attending church last Sunday had been even more awkward than hiding at the ranch during Lacie's riding lessons. He'd planned

to sit somewhere else, but Clay had waved him to the regular pew. So he'd sat at one end and Lacie at the other.

After church, Rayna invited him to Moms, and he'd sat there torturing himself, stealing glances at Lacie. Hadn't quite figured out what was worse yet, seeing her or not. The week at his parents' house had been only slightly easier. Maybe he should move home.

She was here, setting out canning jars filled with peaches, salsa, and a host of other contents he couldn't figure out.

"Hey." He pulled the brim of his hat low. Maybe he could hide how much he'd missed her. But it was probably right there in his eyes.

"Hey." She cleared her throat. "I wondered if you'd still come."

"If I commit to do something, I do it." No matter the cost to his heart. "How can I help?"

"Unload boxes for now."

He emptied a box filled with bags of hulled pecans, jars of assorted jams, and containers of fresh pumpkin pies. The mournful whistle of the freight train in the distance made him miss her even more. Minutes later, it rumbled past, stealing all chance of conversation.

Once the festival officially opened, they barely had time for awkwardness. They bumped elbows, stepped on toes, and brushed against each other filling customer orders all day—with the scent of her perfume making him dizzy. As their shift ended, she was jumpy, as if she couldn't wait to flee. And all he wanted was to settle her down with a kiss.

But then, that would only stir things up.

Though having her near him was torment, he wasn't ready to let her go just yet. He took a deep breath. "Lunch at Moms?"

"Clay's mom has Max. I need to go get him."

He checked his watch. "Shouldn't he be down for a nap about now?"

"You're right. I'll grab something at home and then go get him."

"Listen Lacie, I don't want us feeling uncomfortable around each other."

"It's not gonna work." She propped her hands on her hips.

"I'm not talking about making us work. I'm talking about being friends."

"That's what I mean, the friends thing." Her voice cracked. "It won't work."

"Why?"

"It's a ploy men use. Clay played the friends card with Rayna. Then Stetson pulled the same thing with Kendra. Men pretend to want to be friends, so they can worm their way into a woman's heart. But my heart is officially closed." She smacked herself in the chest. "At least until Max is grown."

Quinn lowered the brim of his hat. "So there's still hope. I've already waited almost ten years for you, what's a few more? Can we share lunch if I promise not to do any worming for another sixteen years?"

She laughed. "You're a nut."

Yes he was. Nutty over her. What she didn't realize was he'd like to win her heart sooner—but if he had to wait until Max was grown—he would. Maybe in another sixteen years, he'd find the courage to tell her the truth. And maybe by then, she could handle it.

"Shall we?" He offered his arm.

"Oh all right. But no touching. Touching is worming."

He held both palms up in a hands-off gesture and followed her to Moms.

They placed their orders and found a small table.

"Why, you little rascal," a young mom gently chided her toddler. "You stole a flag off the Christmas tree when we walked by."

The little girl clasped a small American flag in one plump

hand while her mother tried to pry her fingers loose. "It's not ours. We have to put it back."

The toddler let go, and they headed back to the tree.

Decorated in red, white, and blue, miniature flags, Statue of Liberty ornaments, and stars. Larger flags surrounded the top. "Is it just me, or did I miss Thanksgiving?"

"They put it up for Christmas on Main." She moved her silverware as the waitress brought their teas.

"You going to your folks for Thanksgiving?"

"Yes. We were hoping to get Mama and Daddy in the new house before Thanksgiving." She emptied two yellow packets in her glass; her spoon clinked against the sides as she stirred. "Thanks to you and some good friends, we managed. Don't guess I'll ever need to head to San Antonio again. You?"

"I'm thinking about it. It was great seeing my parents last week. I hadn't been home in a few years."

"Why? You and your folks always seemed close."

Yes, but a certain cowboy had died, and Quinn couldn't face them with his failure. It all seemed silly now. Where else could a cowboy go after failure, other than God and home? Yet he'd turned away from both.

At least Lacie had gotten him on the right track there. Now he had to figure a way to worm his way into her heart, without her knowing he was worming.

For one thing, Max was off limits. Maybe if he kept the focus on just the two of them, she'd lighten up and let him in.

"Quinn?"

He snapped to attention. Lost in thought, lost in her beauty. "What?"

"Why had it been so long since you were home?"

He cleared his throat. "Too busy, I guess."

The waitress set their sandwiches in front of them. "Here we are. Need anything else?"

Lacie shook her head.

"We're fine." He reached for her hand.

She wagged a finger at him. "Touching?"

"Praying."

Red blotches crept up her cheeks. "Oh. Of course."

Her hand slid into his. It felt good. Focus. "Dear Lord, thank You for all Your blessings. Thank You for bringing Lacie back into my life. Keep her and Max safe and happy. Help us to follow Your will. To be Your hands and feet. To reach out to others and glorify You in all we do." His heart pricked. The truth would glorify God. "Bless this food in Jesus' name. Amen."

Lacie's eyes were too shiny. "That's the first time I ever heard you pray."

"I'm ashamed of that."

"Don't be. It's never too late."

And never too late for the truth. "What were we talking about?"

"I don't have a clue."

"Me, neither." All he knew was he sat across the table from her, withholding the truth. And not touching her was killing him.

"Oh, we were talking about your visit home. I always liked your mom. Made everybody feel right at home. I remember our graduation party. She hugged all the kids like they were hers."

"She hasn't changed. Still sells Avon. She asked about you. Wanted to know if you were still barrel racing."

She laughed. "I guess you told her once every five years or so."

"Are you still training Copper over at Clay's?"

"When I decided to board her there again, he made me promise I would."

"I want to see you at the Stockyards this week." He tapped the navy tablecloth for emphasis. "A talent like yours shouldn't be wasted. You showed up once after five years and took second place. I want to see you win."

"No pressure." She rolled her eyes.

"Do I need to sic your dad on you? Me and him, we're like this." Quinn crossed his index and middle fingers. "Tight. Your folks practically had us married off at the mall."

She took a bite of her sandwich, probably uncomfortable with the change in subject.

"Star and Wyatt, too. Are they still seeing each other?"

"They're getting along really well."

"Uh oh. That's bad."

"Why?" Lacie frowned.

"We were getting along well, and then boom, we can't even be friends."

She searched his eyes.

Did she see the pain there?

"I'm sorry, Quinn." She covered his hand with hers. "I just need some time."

He jerked his hand away and held them both up in a back-off stance. "For the record, I had nothing to do with that touching incident."

Lacie laughed—down to her toes. Her face contorted on the verge of hysteria.

"You okay?" Quinn joined in her laughter. "I didn't think it was that funny."

"Fine." Her voice came out too high-pitched. "I haven't laughed like that since Mel died." Her laughter died as quickly as it had come.

"How about a carriage ride, and then we could tour all the other craft booths?"

"Are you worming?"

"Me? I'm highly insulted. I am absolutely not worming. It just looks like fun."

"Well, in that case, let's go."

"The Mustard Seed looks like an interesting Christian bookstore, and I'd like to check out Jackie's Hardware later." And worm his way into spending the day with her.

He was definitely worming. He just had to keep her from realizing it and hope Lacie's locked-up heart would succumb to his brand of charm.

Quinn's steps sped, eager to claim the seat beside Lacie on the long pew.

Back off, Remington. Don't make a point to sit by her. He slowed.

That's it, let Clay and Rayna end up between them. At least Lacie wasn't as stiff around him. More relaxed and friendly since they'd spent most of yesterday together.

If he ever wormed his way into her heart, he'd borrow Clay's hansom cab and take her for a real carriage ride. Their hands-off ride yesterday hadn't done his feelings for her justice.

With Wyatt and Star in attendance, their friends' row was on the verge of filling more than one pew. And everybody in the pew was half of a couple, except him and Lacie. Wyatt and Star were awfully cozy. If only he and Lacie could be.

Slow down, Quinn. Don't push. Give her space. Focus on the sermon. He zoned in as Brother Timothy closed and the music for the altar call began.

Quinn went and knelt there. "Lord, I can't focus on anything but Lacie. I'm sorry. Help me either get over her or win her love. Help me find the right moment to tell her the truth. Thank You for easing my burden about Mel's death, and help Lacie understand when I find the courage to tell her." He stood and returned to his seat.

A deacon closed the service, and the congregation filed out of the pews.

Lacie leaned around Rayna and Clay. "You coming to lunch at Moms?"

"Sure." His heart and face went slack. Like a lovesick puppy, he'd follow her anywhere.

At least get rid of the goofy grin, Remington. But he couldn't.

"We're having a birthday party for my bride." Stetson put his arm around Kendra's waist. "Saturday, December 5th, at six. You're both invited. No gifts, just your presence."

"And no black balloons." Kendra rolled her eyes. "Despite what this clown's told everyone, I'm only twenty-seven."

Lots of opportunities to spend time with Lacie. Things were looking up.

Quinn's traitorous eyes kept pinging back to Lacie as she worked with a student in his arena.

He and Trent had inspected the fences on the entire ranch, and he'd hoped to stay gone until she left, but no such luck. Growling stomachs forced them to the house. He handed the horses over to the groomer and ambled to the house with Trent in step beside him.

"Want to come to the house for lunch? I made chili last night."

"Thank you, Mr. Quinn. I'd be obliged."

Trent had adopted Quinn's words and phrases over the last month. His heart warmed.

He'd tried to help people in the past, been taken advantage of and unappreciated, but Trent wasn't like that.

"You know you're shaping up to be one of the best ranch hands I've ever had. Hardworking, and you keep the cabin spotless."

"I appreciate you taking me in."

"You got a girlfriend?"

"No sir. I used to be a player before I met Jesus. Got a kid somewhere out there."

Quinn swallowed. "You don't know where?"

"Nope. Don't even know if it's a boy or a girl. But I wonder…"

"What?"

"The girl I got pregnant used to be in the youth group." Trent pulled off his work gloves and stuffed them in his coat pocket. "But she moved off and decided to put our kid up for adoption. Six months later, Stetson and Kendra adopted Danielle."

Quinn tried to keep a straight face. Coincidental timing, but could it be true? "How do you feel about being a father?"

"Too young and stupid. Lynn—that's the girl—made the right choice. We were both too young. But I like watching Danielle sometimes."

Quinn clapped him on the back. "Sounds like you've done some growing up."

"Stetson told me Lynn's family's moving back to town. I hurt her bad. She was a good Christian girl. She didn't want to—I talked her into it. I told her I loved her—even though I didn't know what love meant. I'd like to make it up to her somehow."

"I imagine she's hurting over having to make such a tough choice. Maybe you can be her friend."

"Maybe. I definitely won't push her for anything else."

Maybe Quinn could learn from this teenage boy. Maybe he could be what Lacie needed. A friend.

He put his arm around Trent's shoulders.

Trent stiffened and then winced and shrugged away from Quinn.

"What's wrong, son? You hurt?"

"My uncle's removing my tattoos for me."

"I hope your uncle's a doctor."

"He is. I'm keeping antibiotic cream on them like he said, but they feel kind of raw."

"You should've told me. I imagine carrying saddles and tack aggravated the problem."

"I won't shirk my responsibilities around here. And it takes several laser treatments, so it's not a one-time thing."

"Let's light into that chili, and then you're taking the rest of the day off."

"But—"

"No arguing with the boss, boy."

Trent's mouth clamped shut. "Yes, sir."

"I'm thinking of heading to San Antonio this week for Thanksgiving. Visit my folks. Want to ride with me?"

"That's right nice of you, sir. But I don't want to intrude on a family thing."

"You're welcome to join us. My folks would love it." He couldn't leave Trent alone on a holiday, and maybe if he brought a guest, Dad wouldn't get the chance to ask if he'd told Lacie the truth.

"I've never been to San Antonio. Reckon I don't have any other plans."

"Good. We'll head out tomorrow." Quinn stole one more glance at the arena.

And caught her. She was looking at him, too.

He grinned.

Her gaze darted away.

Lacie giggled. Black balloons decorated Stetson and Kendra's house. The cake was done in black roses with thirty candles strategically placed. But Kendra was a good sport about all the teasing.

"Blow 'em out before the whole house goes up in flames." Stetson goosed his wife in the ribs.

"You won't believe what just happened." Star clasped Lacie's hands. Her sister's blue eyes danced.

"What?"

"Wyatt and I went out to the barn to pick a kitten for him to take home. He asked me to marry him."

"What? You barely know each other."

"I knew you'd say that." Some of Star's inner light died. "We've been dating almost three months."

A mere matter of ninety days. She thought the world of Wyatt. But she didn't want to see her sister get hurt again. "You have to admit, that's not very long."

"Yes, but I've been married before, and Wyatt was no saint. It's hard for us to just date."

"So, you wanna get married so you can have sex?" Lacie whispered.

"Of course not." Insulted hurt echoed in Star's tone. "But we want to do things right. I dated Michael for two years, and I'm more sure about Wyatt than I was him. Except—"

"What?"

"We're both Christians, and we're crazy about each other." Star's smile lit the room. "I love Hannah as if she were my own, and we want to have a couple more, too. But Wyatt's been with a lot of women. Do you think I'll be enough to last him the rest of his life?"

"Have you ever looked in the mirror? You're gorgeous." How could Star be so beautiful, so sweet, and lack confidence in herself? "Don't you know when you walk into a room, men stare?"

"You were the beauty queen." Star's shoulders sagged. "Not me."

"I never wanted any of that. I wanted to race barrels. And you didn't. Trust me, that's the only reason you didn't end up on the beauty queen circuit. Besides, what's really important is inside." She clasped her hand to her heart. "Your insides are beautiful. You're the most giving, caring woman I know. If Wyatt really loves you, you'll be enough. Just make sure he really loves you."

Star nodded. "He treats me like a queen and wants to spend all his free time with me. How else can I know?"

"Give it time." Lacie squeezed her hand. "And pray about it."

"I've been praying about it, and if we give it time, we'll

have to go on double dates. You and Quinn want to make a foursome with us?"

"Quinn and I—" Her gaze snagged on his across the room. "We're not dating."

"Well, you should be. You two are nuts about each other. And he's a great guy, Lacie. God's giving you a second chance at love by placing a second stand-up kind of guy in your life. You really shouldn't pass up a gift like that." She lowered her voice. "Don't tell anyone about the proposal. Especially not Mama and Daddy."

Lacie did a zipper motion across her lips like they had done when they were kids. She glanced in Quinn's direction, and her gaze darted away. Why wouldn't he stop staring at her? She sped down the hall, grabbed her coat, and snuck out the back door.

The barn drew her with its hulking promise of peace. A charcoal-gray mama cat meowed at her. Six babies fought for milk, and the mama looked like she needed a vacation.

Lacie picked up the fattest of the kittens and pushed the runt in its place. The fat kitten meowed its annoyance. She sat on a hay bale and cuddled it against her shoulder, scratching its cheek. The kitten changed its tune with a steady rumbling purr.

"You okay?" Kendra leaned in the doorway.

"Just getting some air. Why are barns always so peaceful?"

"The smell of manure, I guess."

"Tell me about Wyatt."

Kendra frowned. "I thought you were interested in Quinn."

"I'm not interested in anyone, but my sister is seeing Wyatt, and they're getting pretty serious."

"Well, he used to be worthless." Kendra settled beside her on the hay bale. "We had an unhealthy, downright lewd relationship before we found the Lord."

"I'm sorry. I didn't mean to bring up a painful subject."

"It's in the past." Kendra waved her hand through the air.

"After I got saved and began seeing Stetson, Wyatt tormented us with my past. But then Stetson rescued him from a bull, and he started changing. A few months later, God got a hold of him, and he's a different person. I often have a hard time reconciling the guy I used to know with who he is now. He probably thinks the same of me."

"What about Natalie?"

"He hasn't heard from her since she signed the papers and handed Hannah over to him."

"Did he love her?"

"He thought he did." Kendra shook her head. "But I think he just wanted to. He'd been convicted about how badly he'd been living and wanted to make things right. Natalie was pregnant, he wasn't even sure if the baby was his, and he wanted to clean things up. I've never heard him mention missing her."

"So he doesn't even know if Hannah is his?"

"He does now. They did a paternity test. But he was willing to take her, even if she wasn't, rather than see her aborted."

The mama cat stood, obviously tired of the feeding frenzy. Kittens fell off as she walked, meowing their discontent.

"Poor overworked mama." Kendra scooped her up.

Lacie set the fat kitten down and ran her fingers through the mama's silken fur. "I've definitely seen changes in Wyatt. You haven't seen any false steps or backsliding?"

"No. I mean he's not perfect. But talking Natalie out of aborting Hannah and raising her himself, that gives him major points in my book. He's focused on doing right by his little girl."

"Speaking of little girls, are you feeling better about Lynn coming back?"

"Her folks came for a visit this week. They held Danielle and played with her. It was nerve-wracking. But they left without her." Kendra hugged herself. "I think one of these

days, God's going to remember who I used to be, everything I did, and take Danielle away from me as my punishment."

Had He taken Mel to punish her for lying to him?

Lacie shivered, put her arm around Kendra, and gave her an encouraging squeeze. "Thank goodness, He doesn't work that way."

"Ahem." The setting sun traced Quinn's silhouette in the doorway. "Stetson's looking for his birthday girl."

Kendra set the mama cat down, jumped up, and brushed off the seat of her jeans. "You both know I'm only twenty-seven, don't you?"

"If you say so." Lacie laughed as Kendra left them alone.

Alone with Quinn.

The kittens closed in on the mama cat. She squatted, scanned the gate of a stall, and leapt up on top of it.

"Not a very nurturing little mama, is she?" Lacie stood, eager to escape.

"There's just nothing like a barn." Quinn closed the gap between them. "Especially an old one, like this."

"A good place to think."

He tipped her chin up with gentle fingers. "And romance."

Chapter 13

Lacie's breath caught. Step back. Run for the house. Her eyes closed.

Quinn's lips touched hers. A whisper of a kiss. His arms came around her, pulling her close.

Her palms rested on his chest. His heart beat steady under her fingertips. Her hands moved up his shoulders and curved around his neck.

The kiss deepened. His lips tasted hers, soft, tender, yielding. His breathing ragged.

He pulled away, stiffened, and set her away from him. "I'm sorry—I shouldn't have done that. But I've wanted to for almost ten years. I'm sorry."

Lacie spun away from him and ran. Darkness had fallen like a curtain. Blindly, frantically, she managed to find her SUV in the glow of the porch light. As she tore out of the drive, she risked a glance at the barn. She could barely make out Quinn's dark shape in the doorway. A living, breathing

man who possessed the power to steal her heart from Mel. The only man she'd ever pledged it to—until death did they part.

Lacie hurried down the hall from the nursery, intent on making it to the sanctuary on time. Another new nursery worker had thrown Max for a loop, and he'd been clingy, but the woman won him over after a few minutes, and he let Lacie leave. Maybe she should volunteer for the nursery and avoid Quinn.

Especially after that kiss. Her fingers went to her lips. Her heart went into overdrive just thinking about it. Oh Mel. How could she enjoy kissing another man so much while she still wore Mel's rings?

She turned the corner.

Kendra stood facing the wall, bumping her forehead against it.

"Kendra?"

Her friend whirled around. "Hey."

"What's wrong?"

"Lynn's here today." Kendra closed her eyes. "They're going to come clean with the church about Lynn's pregnancy."

Lacie's hand flew to her chest. "And who Danielle is?"

"They say they won't reveal that part, and Lynn swears she knows she's too young to be a mom. Says we're Danielle's parents and she's planning to go off to college."

"That's great."

"Yeah, sounds like it." Kendra drew in a shaky breath. "But deep down inside, I just want to grab Danielle out of the nursery, find Stetson, and run as far as we can. Just in case."

Lacie put her hand on Kendra's shoulder. "Understandable. But I don't think it's necessary."

"I hope not."

Even though Quinn itched to be near Lacie, he didn't sit by her. Tension rolled off her.

He shouldn't have kissed her, but he was only human. A man at that. And she'd stood there and closed her eyes like she wanted him to. Ten years was asking a lot of anyone.

Stetson sat beside him. Seemed antsy this morning. Him and Kendra both.

Despite the strain roiling around him, Quinn managed to concentrate on the sermon.

After the altar call closed, Brother Timothy stood. "We have some special friends here today. Brother Luke Watson, his wife, Maggie, and their daughter, Lynn. They moved away and are relocating near Austin. Brother Luke would like to address the congregation."

The man stepped up to the microphone. Stetson stiffened.

"A few years back, I relocated my family to Denver for a job transfer. The truth is, I orchestrated that job transfer."

"To cover up"—his daughter spoke into the microphone—"my pregnancy."

Silence echoed through the congregation. The girl blushed.

Quinn's heart ached for her. This was Trent's ex-girlfriend. So young, so fragile. Danielle's mother. No wonder Stetson and Kendra were so tense.

Her father took the microphone. "What Lynn says is true. I was angry at Lynn and at myself. I felt like I'd failed her as a father. I was a deacon of this church, and I should have been honest.

"Instead, I insisted Lynn's pregnancy be kept a secret. We moved and homeschooled our daughter. No one in Denver even knew she was pregnant. When the baby was born, Lynn signed papers to put our grandchild up for adoption."

"Today, I want to say I'm proud of my daughter." Luke's gaze riveted on something at the back of the church. He cleared his throat.

"She made a mistake, but the baby wasn't a mistake. Our grandchild deserved a good life with Christian adoptive parents, and we were able to do that. We decided to move back

home and come clean. Lynn will be starting college next semester. I hope you'll all keep our family in your prayers."

A smattering of applause moved through the congregation and shouts of "Welcome home." A deacon dismissed the service. Stetson cut around Quinn and left the pew.

Stetson made it to Trent's side as Luke Watson headed in that direction. Quinn hurried to his young tenant.

Luke Watson glared at Trent. "You stay away from my daughter." The words came through clenched teeth.

"Now, Luke, settle down." Stetson's calm tone cajoled. "Trent found the Lord after y'all left."

"He's a good boy, Mr. Watson." Quinn offered his hand.

Luke frowned. "And you are?"

"Quinn Remington. Trent lives on my ranch and works for me. He's turning his life around."

"I know I hurt Lynn." Trent swallowed hard. "And I'm sorry. If I could take it all back, I would."

"Just stay away from her." Luke stalked away.

Kendra and Lacie joined them.

"Everything okay?" Kendra's voice shook.

Stetson nodded. "Let's go get our daughter and go home."

"Trent, you okay?" Lacie's soft tone, like a soothing balm.

"Fine."

"Why don't you come to lunch with Max, Quinn, and me?"

"Can I see you for a second?" Quinn whispered.

"You're looking at me." She grinned.

He took her elbow and pulled her out of Trent's earshot. "I thought you were avoiding me. Especially after… But now you're including me in lunch."

"I just want to make Trent feel better."

"So this isn't about us?"

"I don't know."

He shifted his weight from one foot to the other. "You don't know?"

"All I know is—you confuse the life right out of me."

"Right back at you." He grinned.

"But right now, we have a hurting boy on our hands. Let's focus on him." She walked back to where Trent stood waiting.

"So are we on for lunch?" Her gentle hand patted Trent's shoulder.

Trent winced.

"What's wrong?" She jerked her hand away.

"Trent had his tattoos removed."

"Oh honey, I've heard that's even more painful and expensive than getting them."

"It didn't cost me either way." Trent shrugged. "My dad's a tattoo artist, so he put them on. After I got saved, I didn't want them anymore. My uncle's a doctor, so he took them off."

"Except pain." Lacie patted his hand. "Both times. What a brave young man you are."

"Tell me about this uncle." Quinn shrugged into his coat. "Not that I don't enjoy having you at the ranch, but why didn't he take you in when your dad kicked you out?"

"He always treats me nice, but he has a reputation to uphold. Nice car, fancy house, uptown wife." Trent's shoulders slumped. "Guess I don't fit in, but he sends me money sometimes."

"Well, I think you're a special boy, Trent." Lacie touched his cheek. "I'm proud of you. Just in the short time I've been at this church, I see a change in you."

"Thanks, Miss Lacie." Red splotches stained Trent's cheeks, and he vaulted ahead of them, toward Quinn's truck.

Lacie stopped at her SUV. "And you are, too, Quinn."

"What's that?"

"You're a special man for taking Trent in. I'm impressed with you."

She'd definitely made an impression on him. Especially on his heart. He could stand here all day, just looking at her. With his mouth hanging open.

He clamped it shut, cleared his throat, and forced his feet

into motion. "Better get him home. I hope there's a rain check on that lunch. When Trent's feeling better."

"We'll see." She smiled.

And her smile was enough to keep him going for another week. If only he could spend Christmas with her. Maybe next year.

Maybe never.

A knock sounded at Lacie's door. Max didn't usually wake from his nap, but she hurried to answer just in case, and swung the door open.

Quinn. Her heart stopped then vaulted into double time.

"Do you have a tree yet?"

"No, I haven't gotten around to it."

He stepped aside.

Trent stood behind him, holding a perfectly cone-shaped tree.

She clapped her hands. "It's perfect."

"We were repairing a fence over at my place and saw it. I already have mine up, but I thought of you."

"I'm glad you did. My fake one's in Clay and Rayna's attic, and I didn't want to bother them with it."

"I'll let Trent set it up for you."

"I don't have a stand."

"Got one of those, too."

"You can come in. Max is napping." She pressed her finger to her lips and stepped aside.

Quinn and Trent wrestled the tree through the doorway.

Lacie's heart swelled. Max would love it.

A few quiet minutes later, the tree stood in its stand with fresh water.

"Thanks, Trent." Quinn opened the door. "You can go on down to the truck. I'll be there in a minute."

"Yes, sir. Merry Christmas, Miss Lacie."

"Merry Christmas, Trent. And thank you."

The boy descended the stairs.

Quinn sat down on the landing.

"Thank you." Lacie settled beside him. "This place doesn't feel like home, and I can't seem to get in the spirit of Christmas. But Max needs a tree. He'll be so excited."

"It's only ten days until Christmas. You could get away with putting lights on it, but for my peace of mind, could you put the lights in the window instead of on the tree?"

"Sure. I'd probably worry about fire, too."

"I brought you something else." He dug inside his coat and drew out a gold-foil wrapped box.

Too big for a ring. And too deep for jewelry. Thank goodness. Her heart fluttered with a mixture of joy and disquiet. "I didn't get you anything."

He caught her hand and traced her wedding rings. His hand jerked away. "Sorry. I just broke the touching rule."

He'd done that long ago. Not only had he touched her hand and her lips a few weeks ago, but he'd also touched her heart.

"You have to take it. It's one of a kind and nonreturnable." He placed the box in her hand. "I've noticed you don't seem to know what to do with your rings. I had an aunt whose husband died, back when I was still at home. After a couple of years, my father ordered her one of these. Open it."

Lacie's fingers shook as she tore away the paper then opened the white box. A heart-shaped wedding picture of her and Mel stared from the top of a silver-filigree keepsake box. Her vision blurred.

"I got the picture and date from Star. Hope you don't mind."

She blinked several times and read the inscription: *I'll always remember.* Her fingers traced the engraved words above the picture and their names and wedding date beneath it.

"No pressure, and I'm totally not worming." Quinn's breath stirred the hair at her temple. "I mean it. It's your decision, and it doesn't have anything to do with me. But I figure one

day, you'll get ready—really ready—to take off your rings. And you'll need somewhere special and safe to keep them."

Lacie clasped the box to her heart. "Thank you."

"You're welcome." He stood and offered his hand.

She accepted his help and threw her arms around him. "I'll always treasure it."

"I'm glad." He hugged her back for a moment and then set her away from him and caught a tear tracing down her cheek with his thumb. "I'd better go. We've both broken the touching rule a few times today."

Her laugh came out soggy.

"Now quit crying. I can't leave you standing here crying."

She nodded as he descended the stairs.

At the bottom he shot her a quick grin. "Merry Christmas, Lacie."

"Merry Christmas."

He stepped out of her sight.

She settled on the landing again, tracing her fingers over the most special gift she'd ever received.

Take off her rings now?

No. Not yet.

High in the announcer's booth, Quinn scanned the barrel lineup. Lacie—back in the competition.

She'd been stiff after their kiss then loosened up when her focus had shifted to their friends' problems. But he was pretty sure he'd won her over with his gift. In fact, he could've capitalized on it and stolen a kiss, but he'd promised no pressure. Besides, he didn't want her to think his gift had any strings.

He'd stayed away during her lessons and hadn't seen her except at church for almost two weeks. And since a few of her younger students had cancelled for the winter months, she wasn't at his ranch as much.

Oh how he'd wanted to call her all week and ask her out, but he hadn't dared. Had longed to ask her to drive to his

folks' house on Christmas Eve. Instead, he'd made the trek with Trent. Maybe if he didn't push, things might fall into place with her.

The rider flew off the bronc and landed in the arena below. Quinn snapped to attention. The cowboy jumped to his feet, and Quinn let out the breath he'd been holding.

A vivid reminder of exactly why he shouldn't call Lacie.

"It looked like a fine ride by"—he searched the lineup for the name—"Austin Parker. But things get hairy quick around these parts. Let's give Austin a big hand."

"Next up, barrel racing, starring the finest little fillies in Texas and some mighty fine cowgirls, too."

Lacie was last. He went on autopilot, announcing without his heart in it. Until Lacie entered the arena.

"This cowgirl went a long time without riding. A crying shame, I tell you. But she's back. Let's see what she can do. And…she's off. Around the first barrel in record time."

As Lacie rounded the third barrel, her horse tripped.

Quinn's heart pounded. "Hang on, cowgirl." Catch her if she falls, Lord.

She sailed off the horse, sideways. Her head hit the dirt first.

Chapter 14

Quinn vaulted from the announcer's chair and took the stairs two at a time down to the arena.

By the time he got there, Wyatt and Stetson were walking her out of the arena. Teary-eyed and in obvious pain, Lacie waved. The crowd cheered.

"You need to get back up to the booth." Stetson, in full greasepaint, grabbed Quinn's arm.

"Not until I see she's okay. What hurts?"

"My shoulder." She winced. "But I don't think anything's broken."

An EMT met them at the gate and settled Lacie in a chair.

She followed the medic's instructions, raising her arm as high as she could—not even shoulder level—and pain pinched her delicate features. "You'll need to see a doctor, ma'am."

"I'm not in that bad a shape. Y'all are here for life-threatening emergencies."

"All the same ma'am, I think a trip to the ER is in order."

Lacie shook her head. "I can get myself there."

"I'll take her," Star said.

Quinn supported Lacie as she stood. "I'll drive."

"You need to get back to work, Quinn." Stetson was like an annoying mosquito buzzing around his head. "The second round of bulls is up next."

"They'll fire you," Wyatt said. "I'll go."

"You can't." Star grabbed his arm. "You've got a bull to ride. You'll lose your entry fee."

Quinn cradled Lacie to him. His lips were mere inches away from hers. Within kissing distance. He stole a sweet kiss. Her lips tasted dusty and of blood. "I'm going with you."

"No. I'm fine. Really. Just a little bunged up. You stay."

"I can't. You're more important to me. Let 'em fire me. I really don't care. Besides, my backup's here."

"I'll pull Monty out of the crowd. Go." Stetson smacked him on the back.

Lacie winced and eased her left arm into the sling; the nurse adjusted it. "Your sister has your instructions. Rest, ice packs, and the sling for the first few days, but get moving after that, so you don't get stiff. Got it?"

"Yes, ma'am."

"Now there's a certain cowboy out there—driving all the nurses nuts, wanting to see you."

"Tell him I'll be right out." Lacie fished her lipstick and compact from her purse and made a face at the bruises reflected in the mirror. "Better yet, tell him to leave, and I'll see him next week when I look better."

Quinn had been patient with her. He'd proven his love over and over. He'd left his announcer's booth, right before the most important event of the evening, to be with her. Because she was hurt. It was time to reward him for his devotion. To make a decision. No turning back.

She twisted the rings on her finger. To move forward with Quinn.

*   *   *

Quinn shifted to one side to let the nurse pass and caught a glimpse of Lacie through the open door. "You're beautiful."

"No I'm not." Lacie turned pink. "My cheek's all purple, and my lip's cut."

"You look like you lost a fight with a rodeo arena." Star headed for the door. "Bring her out when she's ready, Quinn. Wyatt's here now. We'll take her home."

"Y'all can go. I'll give her a ride."

Star stopped and turned to Lacie. "That all right with you?"

Lacie nodded.

The door closed behind Star.

"My life flashed before my eyes tonight." Her voice broke. "Copper tripped, and I saw Max without any parents. I prayed all the way to the ground that I wouldn't break my neck like Mel."

"I'm sorry I didn't get there quick enough to catch you this time." He sat in the chair beside the hospital bed and took her good hand in his. "But I prayed for God to catch you, and I firmly believe He did."

"Me, too." She sniffled. "Think you'll get fired?"

"My backup was in the stands."

"You shouldn't have left. I was fine." She moved to stand and winced.

"I can see that. Easy. Take it slow." He helped her up, supporting her good shoulder. "I couldn't stay when my heart was here. When you fell, my life flashed before my eyes, too. My life without you."

Her good arm came around his waist. Her precious, bruised cheek leaned into his shoulder.

"I know I promised not to worm, but I don't want a life without you." Quinn gently embraced her, oh so careful not to hurt her shoulder. "I love you, Lacie. I always have."

Her head tilted back, and she looked up at him, teary-eyed. "I love you, too. I tried not to, but I do."

His head dipped toward her waiting lips.

"Wait." She pressed a hand against his chest.

He backed off. "What?"

"Would you?" She wiggled the trembling fingers of her left hand, sticking out of her sling.

Her wedding rings. He stared at the glittering diamond and simple gold band, and then met her gaze. "You sure?"

Her chin trembled. "I can't kiss you again until I'm free."

The truth will make you free. He didn't have any rights to her until she knew the truth.

"Honey. You don't have to."

"I'm ready. Please."

But she was hurt. And telling her would hurt her more. Let her heal first. Then he'd tell her.

Gently, he loosened the rings, slid them over her knuckle, and off her fingertips.

Her eyes were too shiny.

"Now, see, you're not ready. There's no rush." He started to push the rings back in place.

Her hand fisted, denying him access.

"Happy tears. I love you, Quinn Remington, and I'm ready to embrace the future. With you."

His eyes squeezed shut. He couldn't tell her right now, after she'd made such a monumental decision. And he couldn't resist her either. He drew her hand to his mouth and kissed the white indention where her rings had been.

Her breath caught.

"Are you sure?"

She nodded.

Their lips met, and fire streaked through his veins. Keep it gentle. Don't hurt her cut lip. She loved him back. His heart sang. They'd have plenty of time for more intense kisses. A lifetime of intense kisses.

"I know you can do better than that." Her good arm curled around his neck.

"I don't want to hurt your lip."

"You make my lip feel better."

He grinned and deepened the kiss.

The door opened, and they sprang apart.

Kendra's eyes widened. "We just wanted to check on Lacie."

Greasepaint still decorated Stetson's face, his eyes ringed by big white circles. But his stare issued a challenge.

"Doc said it's a sprain." Quinn's gaze fell to the floor, not ready to face the challenge just yet. "I'm taking her home."

Let her rest a few days. Get her strength back and the pain eased. Then he'd tell her the truth. He had to. Especially now. He couldn't fully take possession of her heart if his was still bound up in a lie.

It couldn't be good for Bob to demand his presence at Cowtown Coliseum. Quinn didn't need the job and had almost not taken it. But he didn't need his employment record marred by getting fired. He squared his shoulders and knocked on the office door.

"Come in."

With his feet propped up on his massive desk, Bob sat eating a sub sandwich. He moved his feet and scooted his chair in closer to the desk. "Remington, glad you could fit me into your schedule."

"I know I shouldn't have left the rodeo the other night, sir. I wouldn't have if Monty hadn't been in the crowd." Unless Lacie had been seriously injured. "I knew he could take over for me."

Bob set the sandwich down and wiped his mouth with a paper napkin. "It's our policy to always have a backup announcer in case of an emergency. Could you explain your emergency?"

Quinn's insides squirmed. He embraced his feelings for Lacie, but explain to his boss?

"I understand you escorted a fallen barrel racer to the hospital."

"Yes, sir."

"It's also our policy to have emergency personnel on hand for our rodeos. If the barrel racer had been seriously injured, the ambulance would have taken her to the hospital."

"Yes, sir."

Bob opened a file on his desk. "The medics' report says her injury wasn't life threatening. Their report states her sister was in attendance and capable of transporting her to the hospital."

"Yes, sir."

"Do you have a valid reason for leaving the announcer's booth to accompany them?" Bob leaned his elbows on the desk and tented his index fingers.

Quinn swallowed hard. "I'm in love with the injured barrel racer, and I plan to marry her."

"I see." Bob pushed away from his desk and propped up his feet again. "I've been married to the same woman for thirty-five years. If my wife were injured, I'd be gone, no matter what I was in the middle of. But the announcer is on stage, an important part of our rodeo. We can't have our announcers abandoning their posts over a sprained shoulder. It looks unprofessional."

"I understand, sir."

"Good." Bob picked up his sandwich. "You may go."

"Go horsey." Max's arms shot up in the air.

Good thing Quinn rode in the saddle behind him with a firm grip on the reins.

The bay horse circled his arena again and again, her gait so smooth, he and Max didn't even jostle.

Lacie had been pale this morning. He'd probably taken advantage of her, asking if he could keep Max today, while she was too sore to put up much protest. But she sure couldn't

handle an active going-on-three-year-old, and she'd get more rest without him there.

He'd been glad to see Rayna there with her. And with Max occupied for the day, Rayna would be more fully attentive to her patient.

A familiar blue pickup pulled into the drive. Stetson. The engine died, and he leapt from the cab like he had a bone to pick with Quinn.

"Trent. Can you take Max to the barn and show him the baby kittens?"

"Sure." Trent trotted over.

Quinn swung the toddler down. "Keep a close eye on him."

"Yes, sir." Trent set Max down but held his hand in a firm grip.

Quinn jogged over to Stetson's truck. "Come to bawl me out for keeping secrets again?"

"You know, I left the ball in your court." Stetson leaned against his tailgate. "Then when it seemed like things went south with you and Lacie, I decided it didn't matter so much. But that was some kiss Kendra and I walked in on. And I take it, you still haven't told her anything."

"The timing just never seemed right, and then things fell apart." Quinn lowered his hat. "Now that things are back on track, I'm planning to marry her, but not without telling her the truth. Just as soon as she's feeling better, I'll shoot straight with her."

"Kendra and I—we just don't want to see her hurt." Stetson offered his hand.

Quinn clasped it. "Me, neither."

"Brother Stetson," Trent called. He walked toward them, still holding Max's hand.

Stetson shielded his eyes from the sun. "Hey, Trent."

"I have to ask you something, sir." Trent took a steadying breath. "Is Danielle my daughter?"

"Son." Quinn settled a cautioning hand on Trent's shoulder and scooped up Max.

Stetson coughed, as if someone had sucker-punched him.

"I'm not gonna do anything about it if she is." Trent hung his head. "I want to know, so I can have peace about it. She reminds me of me."

"If you ever do anything," Stetson growled, "to let her know before we think she's old enough, or try to take her away from us, you'll deal with me." He jabbed himself in the chest.

"I won't. I swear. I just needed to know." Trent's voice cracked. "I'm glad she has you and Miss Kendra. It's where she belongs."

Stetson looked up at the sky then closed the gap between him and Trent.

Quinn cut between them.

"Relax." Stetson sidestepped Quinn and hugged Trent.

Only three days since she'd fallen off the horse. The sling was off. No more ice packs. Her shoulder was still sore, but no more throbbing pain. She was itching to get outside, but Rayna had made the porch her boundary.

New Year's Eve and she couldn't even go to the watch night at church.

Star sat with her while Wyatt and Clay talked horses in the barn.

"Did you mention your proposal to Mama and Daddy yet?"

"No. I figured they'd freak, like you did."

"We don't want you to get hurt." Lacie moved her arm to a more comfortable position. "But I talked with Kendra about Wyatt, and I'm convinced he's a new man."

"I know they had a thing in the past. His past is the only thing that gives me caution. The only man I've ever been with is Michael."

"That's a good thing. A biblical thing."

"I know, but what if I don't measure up?" Star rolled her eyes. "Kendra is so beautiful."

"So are you. And Wyatt never loved Kendra. He loves you. He offered to forfeit his ride the other night to go to the hospital. Because he loves you."

"I know you're right. But what about Natalie? Did he love her? What if she comes back?"

"After they'd ended their relationship and she'd learned she was pregnant, he accepted Christ." Her shoulder throbbed again, and she repositioned it. "Kendra got the impression he'd seen the error of his ways and wanted to love Natalie. To marry her and make things right with God. But Kendra said he's never mentioned missing her. And if you love someone, you miss them when they're not around."

"I'll tell Mama and Daddy this weekend."

Wyatt ambled into view, and Star ran to meet him. They flew into each other's arms. Wyatt swung Star around in the air, and then they melted into a toe-curling kiss.

"Y'all need to get a room or get married," Lacie called. Might as well take the opportunity to test Wyatt.

Wyatt waved. "I'll take the married option."

"Good. That's my sister, you know."

Star giggled as they climbed into Wyatt's truck.

It was nice to see her sister so happy. In fact, she'd never been that happy with Michael, not even when they first started dating.

A familiar truck pulled into the drive. Lacie's heart revved. Like she was sixteen again—but with a really sore shoulder and stretch marks.

Quinn sauntered toward her.

She ran to meet him. But it jarred her shoulder, so she slowed to a walk.

"Hey, beautiful." He greeted her with a tender kiss.

"Take me for a walk. I'm dying, and Rayna won't let me out of her sight."

His eyes were serious. Something was up. Something that quieted the clatter of her heart right down.

"Rayna's got Max?"

"Yep." She almost didn't want to go now. Had she gotten him fired? "Stetson said you had a meeting with management at Cowtown."

"He called me down for leaving the night you got hurt."

"And?"

"I told him I was in love with you. He's a family man, so he let me slide."

Her shoulders relaxed. His meeting had gone well, so what was bothering him? "Want to sit on the porch instead of walking?"

"No. I'm up for a walk if you're sure you are." His arm encircled her waist; his thumb hooked in her belt loop.

But tension crashed off him.

"Are you okay?"

"I have to tell you something, Lacie. I've needed to for a long time. I want to start this new year right with you."

Chapter 15

Lacie's throat closed up. She swallowed hard. "What is it?"

Music began to play. "Desperado." Quinn's cell.

"That's Trent." He dug the phone from his pocket. "I got rid of that tone—since I'm not lonely anymore—except for his calls. I need to take this."

"Of course."

"Trent. What's wrong? Slow down, son. I can't understand you." Concern etched Quinn's rugged features.

Lacie's stomach twisted.

"I'll call an ambulance and be right there."

Lacie's heart leapt to her throat. "What?"

"He went to see his dad." Quinn punched in 911. "And his dad beat him to within an inch of his life. I have to go now. Get back to the house. Call Stetson and Brother Timothy."

She charged for his truck, gritting her teeth against the pain in her shoulder. "I'm going with you."

"No." Quinn ran alongside her, talking to the operator as

he went. "My friend has been beaten up badly. He's in an alley behind—" Quinn's truck door shut.

She jerked the passenger side open and dove in.

Still talking to the operator, he pointed and waved her out of his truck.

She shook her head.

His engine revved to life, and he tore out of the drive.

Lacie fished her cell from her pocket and dialed Kendra's number.

Quinn jumped out of his truck almost before it stopped rolling, opened Lacie's door, and helped her out. Stubborn woman would reinjure her shoulder before the day was over.

"Didn't I order you out of my truck back at the ranch?"

"You go ahead, I'll catch up."

"You sure?"

She nodded, and he bolted to the hospital entrance.

The emergency lobby was empty. Quinn hurried to the window.

"Quinn Remington. I'm Trent Stevens' friend."

"He's been asking for you." The nurse pushed a button and gestured him to the door. "First room on the right."

The antiseptic smell of the hospital jabbed him in the gut.

A doctor stood by the bed.

Trent's battered face was swollen, his eyes closed. Dried blood lined his upper lip.

Quinn's stomach bottomed out; the backs of his eyes scalded. How could a man do such a thing to his own child?

One of Trent's eyes opened. The other wouldn't. "Hey."

"Hey. You okay?"

Trent tried to smile, but with his misshapen lips, it looked garish. "Dumb question. This is my uncle, Rick."

"Trent's told me a lot about you." Rick pointed at Trent. "You think about college. I'll pay for whatever you want to do with your life. Doctor, lawyer—anything that appeals to you."

Interest stirred in Trent's eyes. "I always kind of wanted to be a vet."

"A fine profession. I'll look into it and get with you." Rick offered his hand to Quinn. "I have to make rounds, but you'll never know how much I appreciate what you've done."

"Having Trent around has been good for me, too." Like a second chance to help Hank.

Quinn waited until they were alone. "What happened?"

"I hadn't seen Dad in a while. I only wanted to visit. Start the new year off right." Moisture seeped from under Trent's swollen-shut eye.

Quinn grabbed a tissue from the box by the hospital bed and gently dabbed away the tear.

"Never mind, you can tell me later."

"No, I'm okay." Trent licked his lips. "He was drunk, and he got mad because I hadn't checked on him sooner."

Guess the loser forgot he'd kicked Trent out.

"I managed to get away from him and ran as far as I could. A couple of blocks."

Quinn's chest steamed. The terror Trent must have felt. "You should have gone to a neighbor's house."

"What if he'd come after me and beat them up, too?"

"You need to press charges."

"Against my dad?"

"Being your dad doesn't give him the right to hurt you."

Trent shook his head. "No. No charges."

The door opened, and Lacie stepped in the room. Her hand flew to her mouth. "Oh, Trent. You poor baby."

"I'm trying to talk him into pressing charges."

"He'd only come after me again."

"Not if he's in jail. And we'd file a restraining order. I can protect you, Trent."

"No."

Lacie gently touched Trent's shoulder. "What if the mail carrier had been there and tried to help you? What if the lady

next door tried to help you? What if Kendra and Stetson decided to check on your dad? If he could do this to you, he could hurt someone else."

"But the Bible says to honor your parents."

"Yes, but parents are supposed to behave in an honorable manner." Quinn's tone boiled.

Lacie shot him a cool-it glare. "The Bible also says to love your neighbor. Your father is a time bomb waiting to go off. What if he hurts some innocent passerby?"

Trent's good eye squeezed shut. "You're right. I'll do it."

Lacie threaded her fingers through Quinn's as they exited the hospital. "Poor kid. Is anything broken?"

"No, just pretty bunged up." He took a deep breath. "You realize things could get ugly with his dad?"

"You think he'll come after you?" Her voice quivered.

Quinn shrugged. "I'll manage, but my ranch is on lockdown where you're concerned until this is over."

"What about my lessons?"

"I called Clay when you went to get coffee. We worked out a schedule for your students' lessons at his arena, once your shoulder's up to it."

"That won't work. Trish has lessons, too."

"Several of her students completed their courses, so your students fit in between hers."

"Don't you think you're taking this a little too far?" She stopped, propping her hands on her hips.

"Last I heard they haven't found Trent's dad yet." Quinn put an arm around her good shoulder and walked her to his truck. "He could come after Trent and whoever happens to get in his way. When they do find him, they'll send him to a dry-out clinic first. After that, he could make bail, and I wouldn't put it past him to try to escape."

"This is crazy. Surely Trent's uncle won't bail him out."

"You never know. He didn't take Trent in when he needed him." He stopped near his truck and traced her jaw with gentle fingertips. "I'll do what I have to—to protect Trent, you, and Max. Hopefully, it'll be over soon, and I'll high-tail it your way just as quick as I can."

Max. She hadn't even thought of her son being in danger. But Quinn had. "I don't want you in danger."

"I won't be."

"I mean it, Quinn. Be careful. I love you. And I can't lose—"

He stopped her words with a tender kiss. "I'll be careful. I love you, too. Enough to keep you safe. How's that arm?"

"A little achy."

"You should have stayed put like I told you. You'll definitely overdo it while I'm not around to keep an eye on you."

"I'll miss you."

"Me, too."

His arms came around her, and she wanted to stay there forever. How would she stay away?

The man she loved lived only a couple of miles down the road, but it seemed like across the country.

A knock sounded on Lacie's door. Nursemaid Rayna at her service. Truth be told, even propped in her bed on a mound of pillows, her shoulder hurt just from the weight of her arm. She loved Rayna for wanting to take care of her, but it was getting old.

"Come in."

Mama stalked into the room. "Your sister wants to get married."

"She's a grown woman."

"But she hasn't had good judgment in the past. I never liked Michael."

"I know."

"Did you like him?"

"No."

Mama crossed her arms over her chest. "I prayed from the time you girls were in my tummy for a good, godly husband for each of you. At least it worked for you—but then we lost Mel."

Lacie's eyes burned. "I appreciate those prayers. But free will comes in there somewhere. She made a bad choice with Michael. Maybe Wyatt is the good, godly man she needs."

"I liked Wyatt from the moment I met him. But they've only known each other a matter of months." Mama's palms jutted upward. "What do we know about this man?"

"I know he's a Christian and he loves Star. If there's one thing a bull rider can't stand, it's forfeiting a ride. When I got hurt at the arena, Wyatt offered to leave before his scheduled ride to go with Star to the hospital. And she didn't even ask him to."

"Do you think Star's ready to be a stepmom?"

"I think she loves Hannah, and Hannah loves her."

Mama sighed and settled on the edge of Lacie's bed. "Maybe Wyatt is the man for her. Now if we could just get you moving forward."

"I'm in love, Mama."

Mama gasped. "With Quinn?"

Lacie laughed. "I didn't think it was that shocking."

"Last I knew you were fighting it tooth and nail."

"He won me over."

"Well, it's about time. He won me over ten years ago." Mama started to hug her then stopped short. "How's that shoulder?"

"Sore."

"We've got to get you well since we've got a wedding to plan by Valentine's. That's only six weeks away. Star's trying to give me a coronary."

* * *

Lacie grabbed the phone on her nightstand on the second ring.

"How's the patient?"

Her insides quivered at the sound of Quinn's voice. "Impatient. But better since you called. How's Trent?"

A whole week had passed since she'd seen him, and his frequent calls barely kept her going.

"Sleeping peacefully in my guest room. Less pain and looking a heap better. He can open both eyes now. Police finally caught up with Trent's dad. He's officially in the treatment center. In fact, while he's there, I've got a proposal for you."

She stood and paced around her bed. Surely he wouldn't propose to her over the phone. Her heart hammered a frantic rhythm. "I'm listening."

"Trent's uncle pulled strings to get him in Texas A&M. I'm driving him down this weekend. With his dad in the treatment center, I feel safe enough for you to ride with us."

A tinge of disappointment weakened her knees. She sank to the bed. At least she'd get to spend some time with him. "I'd love that."

"I was hoping you would. Think your folks could keep Max?"

"I'll check with them. They're reeling from the news that Star and Wyatt are getting married."

"Wow, that was fast."

Not as fast as she'd like to marry Quinn, though. "That's what Mama thought. The wedding's on Valentine's Day. Think you'll be able to make it?"

"Surely things will settle by then, hopefully before. I can't imagine not seeing you for five more weeks."

"Me, neither." Her voice came out sad, lost.

"How's Max?"

"Sleeping, and growing like a dandelion while he does."

"Does he miss me?"

"Asks about you every day."

"That okay with you?"

"I'm glad he loves you as much as I do."

"Being away from you is killing me." His voice caught.

Music to her Quinn-starved ears. He was making her a basket case.

"All these years of loving you, Lacie Maxwell, and I finally get you to love me back, but we can't be together."

"Tell me about it. Will I at least see you at the rodeo?"

"No. The regular announcer has fully recovered. He starts this week. I'm backup to his backup. Monty's covering until further notice."

"Any word on the trial date?"

"Gotta get Trent's dad dried out first. Listen, I gotta rustle up some grub for Trent. Dream of me."

"Always." Quinn had long since replaced Mel in her dreams, so seamlessly she hadn't even realized when it happened.

Quinn stood on the sidewalk surrounded by the perfectly landscaped grounds of Texas A&M. The historic academic building looked like a capitol complex, with its pillared front and domed roof.

Trent hadn't seemed nervous during his and Lacie's grand tour. They'd seen his dorm, the Liberty Bell replica suspended from the dome, and the huge mosaic-tiled university seal in the floor of the rotunda.

All they had left to do—was leave.

"Want us to walk you back to your dorm?" Quinn clapped Trent on the back.

"I know my way around."

"Your uncle certainly doesn't do small." Lacie spun in a circle, surveying the campus, her eyes huge. "I'd get lost—so bad, nobody would ever find me."

"It's supposed to be the best veterinary program in Texas." Trent smiled. "And not so overwhelming, once you get used to it."

"Just wish it wasn't so far from home." Quinn's eyes scalded. "You call, anytime."

"I will."

"I mean it. And any weekend you want to come home, just holler."

"And if he can't come get you, I will." Lacie hugged him.

Trent returned the hug. "Thanks."

"I'm proud of you, son." Quinn lowered his hat.

Lacie let go of Trent.

If Quinn hugged him, he might lose the battle. He hugged the boy anyway. With bone-jarring man claps on the back, they embraced for a long time.

"Thanks for everything, Mr. Quinn. I don't know what I'd have done without you." Trent's voice broke.

"You helped me out, too, boy. More than you'll ever know. Just remember, once you make good on that degree and set up your vet practice in Aubrey, I get a cut rate." Quinn swiped his eyes and let go of him. Like letting go of his own kin.

Lacie's fingers threaded through his. "You'll come to Star and Wyatt's wedding, won't you?"

"I don't know them very well."

"Work with me, Trent. It's an excuse to get you home for a weekend."

"Wouldn't miss it." Trent grinned.

Quinn clamped a hand on Trent's shoulder, his mouth opened.

"I know"—Trent grinned—"stay in church."

Now or never. He had to leave. Trent would be okay here. "Go on now; at least let us make sure you head in the right direction to get back to your dorm."

Trent waved.

Quinn stood watching until he could no longer see him.

"Come on, tough guy. Need a shoulder?"

Lacie's eyes swam.

Quinn's did, too.

He tucked her against his side and headed to the lot where he hoped he'd parked his truck.

Lacie finished with her final student of the day, and the groomer took Copper to the barn.

A few months back, she'd longed to work at Clay's arena again. Now, all she wanted was to be at Quinn's, near him, spending time with him, kissing him. The memory of him taking off Mel's rings with such tenderness and love for her had played over and over in her mind.

"What's that smile about, young lady?" Clay climbed the fence and sat on the top rail. "Have a nice weekend trip, did you?"

Careful not to strain her left arm, Lacie clambered up beside him. "Do you think Mel would like Quinn?"

Chapter 16

Lacie held her breath, awaiting Clay's answer.

"I do. They're a lot alike in some ways. Different in others."

"Do you like Quinn?"

"As long as he's good to you and Max, he's got my vote."

"He is. So this is okay with you?" She traced where her rings had been.

"It's not really my concern."

"We've been through a lot together." She crossed her ankles. "There for a while, when we were traveling to so many Horizon Series rodeos, I spent almost as much of my waking hours with you as I did Mel."

"Thousands of rodeos to success"—Clay adjusted his hat—"and beyond. Even though Mel got heaven out of the deal, I miss him like the dickens. Him dying hurt me almost as much as it did you."

"I know." She sniffled. "Maybe that's why I feel like I need your approval. Like you're my big brother or something."

"Want me to walk you down the aisle or something?"

"That would insult my dad. But I do want you to be there for me."

"Has he asked you yet?"

"No, but once he gets this stuff wrapped up with Trent, it seems to be heading in that direction."

"I'll be there. I'll even wear one of them monkey suits for you."

Tears filled her eyes. "Do you think I'm making Mel sad?"

His arm came around her shoulder. "No, sweetheart. He'd want you to be happy, and he'd want a good daddy for Max. I think Quinn fits the bill on both counts, and Mel would, too."

She leaned into him, nodding against his shoulder. "Remember that time we were in Oklahoma and Mel couldn't find his lucky spurs?"

"I thought he was gonna forfeit his ride over them blasted things. In some ways, he was the orneriest cowboy I ever knew."

Lacie laughed. "Tell me about it. Even though he won that night without them, he still had to wear those spurs for every rodeo after that."

They sat there until dusk, replaying memories of the man they both loved—sharing tears, bursts of laughter, and laughing until they cried.

Quinn was quick to claim the seat beside Lacie in church.

She rewarded him with a big smile. That and her perfume made him dizzy.

"Missed you." He took her hand in his.

"Me, too." Her shoulder pressed against his.

He probably should have given her more room, but he couldn't bring himself to scoot over one centimeter. "Trial's been set. Two weeks from tomorrow."

"Thank goodness." She closed her eyes. "Trent's dad's in jail?"

"So far. I'm surprised his brother didn't bail him out. But I don't trust him to leave Trent's dad there for two more weeks. He's one of the coldest men I've ever met."

"But if he was going to post bail, seems like he would have done it by now."

"I'm not taking any chances with the woman I love. As much as it pains me, I still want you to stay away. But"—he squeezed her hand, dreading what he had to do—"if everything goes according to plan, I want us to spend the Tuesday after the trial together. All day—just you and me."

"I'd absolutely love that. But I can't."

His heart dipped low. "Can't?"

"Star's getting married that week, and I'll be jumping in circles."

"Please don't make me wait another week."

"Trust me." Her gaze spoke volumes. "I don't want to. But I have to help get my sister married off. Mama's about to dissolve into conniptions."

He drew in a deep breath. "How about this? I'll keep Max for you, and we can do some bonding. Maybe even meet you for lunch. After the wedding, I get a day of you to myself, and then we'll spend family time with Max."

"That sounds like a dream. I guess stolen moments in church will have to do until then. Lunch at Moms?"

"I think we could risk that." He winked at her. But the truth gnawed at his insides.

"After the wedding, just give me a date." She winked back.

His heart landed in the toes of his cowboy boots. He was a goner for sure. If only he didn't have to shatter that sparkle in her eyes.

Lacie held Max's hand as they meandered toward her SUV after lunch. Already, he was just too big for her to carry.

Quinn had already left. She wouldn't see him again until Wednesday-night Bible study.

"How about an airplane ride, wrangler?" Clay scooped up Max and ran, sailing her son through the air.

Max giggled all the way to her truck.

"He should be doing that with Kayla."

"Nonsense." Rayna clucked her tongue. "We both love Max, and Clay likes helping you with the car seat. I can still carry Kayla. For the time being." Rayna readjusted her daughter on her hip. "So what's going on with you and Quinn? Y'all look like a pair of lovesick cows."

"Thanks for the pretty picture."

Rayna rolled her eyes. "I think I've spent too much time at the ranch. Rephrase—a pair of lovebirds. There, that's better."

"We love each other."

"Oh, I'm so happy for you." Rayna grabbed her arm, stopping Lacie's progress, and hugged her. "I knew there was another great guy somewhere out there that God would deliver just for you."

"Once this thing with Trent is over, I think we'll be spending a lot of time together, so Max can get to know him better."

"Max already loves him."

"I want them to have plenty of bonding time."

"Has he popped the question?"

"No, but I figure it's coming."

"Oh, I'm so excited for you." Rayna bobbed up and down. "You deserve this, Lacie."

"A couple of years ago, I didn't think I could ever be really happy again."

"God is good. All the time. While you were grieving, he was moving Quinn in your direction and timed it just right to where you'd be ready for a new chapter in your life. Just imagine, he saved Quinn all these years, just for you."

She hadn't really thought of it that way. God quietly working behind the scenes for her and Max. She looked up at the dazzling blue sky. *Thank You, Lord.*

* * *

Quinn didn't know how to act. He couldn't let his ecstasy show. Trent's dad was safely ensconced in jail for a year. But Trent was torn.

"You did the right thing, son."

Trent nodded. But his gaze stayed on the sidewalk as they left the courthouse.

"Wait up, Trent," a man called, several yards behind them.

Trent's uncle jogged to them, his tie loosened and askew. He dug out his wallet. "I know you need more from me than money. And I'm sorry about that. I owe you more."

"It's okay, Uncle Rick."

"No, it's not." He handed Trent a check. "Jessica comes from old money, high society. I definitely married up. And at the time, I think I was enamored with the fact that she was interested in me. I fell hard. She can be difficult—way too concerned with appearances."

"I definitely don't fit in with appearances." Trent's shoulders slumped.

"I don't fit her appearances." Rick clamped a hand on Trent's shoulder. "But we have a daughter, and I can't lose her. Everything I do is to keep Jennifer in my life. Otherwise, I'd take you in. But Jessica gave me a choice, and I—"

"It's okay, Uncle Rick. I understand. I'm fine. Mr. Quinn's been good to me, and I love school. I'm happy where I am."

"I'm proud of you. Against amazing odds, you've grown into a fine young man."

"Thank you, sir." Trent stood a little straighter in his uncle's praise.

Rick hugged his nephew then left them alone.

"Let's get you back to school." Quinn put his arm around Trent's shoulder.

Trent was free. And so was Quinn.

To tell Lacie the truth and hope their future survived it.

* * *

Lacie waited on the landing outside her suite, while Max watched Daffy Duck. Her heart hammered a frantic rhythm. Trent's dad was in jail. Everyone was safe. But she had to concentrate on Star's wedding. After that, her life with Quinn could begin. They'd only have stolen moments for the next week, but happily-ever-after stretched before them.

Quinn bounded up the stairs and rewarded her with a toe-curling kiss. "Wow. I just kissed Lacie Maxwell."

She giggled. "Anytime, sir."

"I wish you could come with us."

"Me, too. But the wedding's on Thursday. We'll spend Friday together. Trish is handling my riding lessons all week, so I'll be free."

"Until Friday then." He kissed her again. "I'd better get Max, or we'll stay here all day."

"I could live with that. One more of those for the road."

"I aim to please." He pulled her close and dipped her backward.

She laughed as he rained sweet kisses over her face.

Quinn sat in the crowded lobby of the Galleria Dallas. The food court made his stomach rumble.

"Look." Max pointed to a little girl gliding across the ice like she was born there.

"Maybe after we eat with your mama, we can try that." He tried to concentrate on the skaters, but waiting for his first glimpse of Lacie was like sitting on saddle burs.

In the distance, she headed his way, dressed in denim, rhinestones flashing in the mall lighting. Her sky-blue shirt made her eyes glow.

"There's your mama." He held Max's hand tight, but his small feet made progress slow. Quinn scooped him up and hurried to meet her.

She flew into his arms.

"Mama, we're gonna skate."

"You are?" She kissed Max's cheek and looked at Quinn like she wanted to kiss him, too. But she didn't.

Quinn hugged her close with Max between them, like a family. Just the way he wanted them to be. Happily-ever-after was within his grasp. If they could only handle his final hurdle.

But they'd deal with that Friday. Today was a fun day. "Italian or something else?"

"Mmm, you speak my language. How about lasagna, Max? Or spaghetti?"

"Sketti."

"I thought we might do some ice-skating after we eat."

Lacie laughed. "If you think you're up to holding us both up."

Her laugh always sounded like an angel chorus. If only he could keep her laughing.

Lacie couldn't stop smiling as Quinn skated around the rink with Max in his arms. Rapt joy washed over Max's little face with every turn. After a few rounds, Quinn set Max down, and then skated backward, holding both of her son's little hands. His laughter echoed across the ice.

She clung to the rail, making slow progress around the rink.

"Hey. You hold Max's hands, and I'll hold you." Quinn zoomed up and placed Max in front of her. His arms came around her waist from behind.

"I'll get my feet tangled up with yours, and we'll all fall."

"No, I've got you. Just hold Max."

They made slow, awkward progress around the rink, with Quinn skating backward, dragging her and Max along. She didn't even try to move her feet. They stayed slightly steadier that way. Luckily, the rink wasn't too crowded in the middle of the day on Wednesday.

"Only two more days and I get you all to myself." Quinn's whisper swept chill bumps over her skin.

Having him so close—hearing Max's laughter, she could definitely spend the rest of her days like this.

"You know I plan on marrying you, Lacie Maxwell."

Her breath caught.

"This isn't my official proposal. Gotta get a ring. Just want you to know my intentions." He nuzzled her ear.

She could die right here and be happy. "I love you." She barely breathed the words, but Max was still giggling and wouldn't have heard anyway.

"You make my days. Soon you'll make my nights."

"You're driving me crazy."

"You've driven me crazy for ten years." He skated her over to the rail.

She grabbed it with one hand.

Quinn scooped up Max and sailed around the rink.

Lacie stayed put and concentrated on getting her breathing back to normal.

Quinn hung around in the hall outside the classroom. Clay's mom had agreed to keep an eye on Max, and Quinn was determined to steal a minute or two with Lacie before the wedding.

Feminine laughter led him to the right door. "Bride's Room—Do Not Enter—Especially if You're the Groom," the sign read. Quinn rapped on the door.

Sudden quiet inside.

"Who is it?" Lacie called.

"Quinn. Can I see you for a second?"

Whistles echoed through the door as it opened.

Lacie's face was crimson, her dress, a pink lace pouf. The most beautiful southern belle he'd ever seen.

He grabbed her hand and pulled her into an empty class-

room. The whistles and giggles echoed behind them, and he closed the door.

"You'd better kiss me before I faint from anticipation."

Quinn's gaze went from her eyes to her lips. A slight smile curved them up. He kissed one corner then the other. She moaned as he took full possession. Pliant in his arms, Lacie Maxwell tasted sweet as honey. His and his alone. They'd have to get married soon.

Only one thing stood between them. The truth. He pulled away from her.

Her eyes fluttered open. "What's wrong?"

"Had to stop while I still could." His voice came out gruff with all he felt for her. And all he had to tell her. "You'd better go back."

"I'm not real sure I can walk."

He offered his arm, careful not to get too close.

"Do you really think it's wise for us to spend the day together tomorrow? Alone? Maybe we should take Max along." She shot him a teasing grin. "Of course that didn't keep you in line at the skating rink."

"It'll be hard, but I'll keep myself under control. Maybe we just won't touch."

"That's no fun." She smiled up at him, and he wanted to kiss her again.

But he couldn't. "You've got a wedding to get to."

"Maybe we could crash Star's wedding and make it a double."

"I want our wedding day to be ours alone." And after tomorrow, she might not want a wedding. Not with him anyway.

"Lacie, you okay?" Star grinned.

"Just a little weak-kneed. Where's Mama?"

"She decided she'd done all she could with me and went to find Daddy."

This was Star's day. Concentrate. Forget Quinn—and his kiss—for the moment.

Star's ivory dress was all Old South. She looked like a kind, blue-eyed version of Scarlett O'Hara. "You're beautiful."

"I hope Wyatt thinks so."

"You're the only woman he's noticed since he met you."

Star hugged her. "I'm so happy."

"I can tell. You're positively radiant."

"Oh Lacie, I hope you can be this happy soon."

"I already am."

Star's left eyebrow shot up.

"Quinn wants me to marry him."

"Oh, that's wonderful." Star clasped her hands together.

"It is." Lacie smoothed her sister's veil. "But today is your day. And I think it's about time for me to find Mama and Daddy."

She hugged her sister close and stepped out into the empty hall.

Quinn spotted Clay in the fellowship hall. No one else was around. He'd been needing to do this. And he was out of time.

"Clay. Just the man I need to see."

"They sent me down to look for matches. Got any ideas?"

"My mama always kept 'em up high in a cabinet."

The two men entered the kitchen and opened and closed cabinet doors.

"Pay dirt." Clay held up a box. "What'd you need to see me about?"

Quinn leaned against the countertop. "I'm crazy about Lacie."

"I reckon the feeling's mutual. You really don't need my blessing, but you've got it."

"That's a relief, but I can't take that blessing. Not until she knows the truth."

Clay scowled. "I was afraid you was too good to be true. What—you're married? I told you not to hurt her."

"It's nothing like that. But I should have told her a long time ago. It also affects you." Maybe if Clay could handle the news, Lacie could, too.

Lacie hurried toward the sanctuary, her heart still in a flutter over Quinn's kiss.

But she had to focus on the wedding. She'd searched everywhere for Daddy with no luck, and it was almost time to start.

Voices drifted from the direction of the fellowship hall. She stopped. A man. Maybe Daddy. Too far away to tell. She headed in that direction.

"Sounds like you better spit it out."

That was Clay. Maybe Daddy was with him.

"It's gonna come as a shock." Quinn's voice.

She should go on to the sanctuary. Find Daddy.

"Try me."

Clay again. Whatever they were discussing was none of her business. But her feet, rooted to the spot, refused to move.

"I used to raise livestock. Does the name"—Quinn's voice broke—"Cactus Red ring a bell?"

Lacie's heart plummeted. No, no, no!

"The last horse Mel rode."

"I raised him. He was my horse."

Quinn's admission shattered her soul.

Chapter 17

Lacie whirled around and ran.

Quinn's horse killed Mel.

And he hadn't bothered to mention that?

She had to get out of here. So she could think. So she could breathe.

She rounded a corner in the hall and ran into something solid. "Daddy."

"You okay, sweetheart?"

Star's day. Pull it together. You can crumble later. "I was just trying to find you and Mama."

"Your mama's in with Star. They sent me to look for you." He checked his watch. "We'd better get back."

She took the arm he offered.

"Sweetheart, you're shaking. Is something wrong?"

"I want everything to be perfect for Star."

"Everybody puts so much stock in the wedding going off without a hitch. It's the marriage that really matters." He patted her hand. "I think Star picked the right fella this time."

She took several deep breaths—just get through this wedding.

"You sure you're all right?"

"I'm fine, Daddy. Star's waiting for us."

Quinn braced himself for the punch Clay looked capable of throwing.

"You should have told us both when you first hit town." Clay's voice was stone cold, rock hard.

"I'm a coward."

"Not necessarily. I imagine it would be a hard thing to live with. A hard thing to tell."

"I sold my business and wallowed in guilt for over two years."

"And then you ended up here. I suspect you knew she lived here."

Quinn nodded. "I wanted to try and help Mel's widow, that's all. Financially, keep her house up, whatever I could do, and help out at your ranch. But I didn't know who she was."

The one that got away. His insides twisted. This time she'd gotten away for good.

"I let my feelings for her get in the way, and I was afraid if I told her, she'd run the other way. If I'd told her to begin with, maybe she wouldn't have fallen in love with me, and I wouldn't have hurt her so badly. But I put it off, hoping I could win her over."

"You really love her?"

"Since high school." Quinn ducked his head. "But she was already in love with Mel when we met."

"You figure she'll blame you for his death?"

"Maybe. I did. For a long time until I got reacquainted with Jesus."

"It's stuck in my craw. And I'll have to chew on it awhile. I loved Mel like a brother."

"I'm sorry."

"But you're not to blame for his death." Clay reached up as if to adjust a hat that wasn't there. "It was an accident. Part of rodeo. It could've happened with any other horse or a bull for that matter. I believe we only get taken out on God's timetable. For whatever reason, it was Mel's day to go home."

Quinn nodded. "It took me a couple of years and getting reacquainted with God to remember that."

"Besides, you didn't train the horse to kill. You trained it to give a good ride, and Mel wouldn't have wanted it any other way."

"I'm glad you feel that way. I respect you, Warren. Always have, even when I kept up with your career on the circuit, before I knew you."

"I appreciate that." Clay offered his hand. "When you gonna tell her?"

Quinn clasped Clay's hand. "Tomorrow. I'd appreciate it if you didn't say anything."

"It's your telling to do. Not mine. But see that you stick with the plan. It's time to come clean, my friend."

Clay still considered him a friend. Maybe Lacie could, too. "I'd appreciate your prayers on the matter."

"Will do. Now I better get these matches up to Rayna, or she'll call the posse."

He'd tell her, first thing in the morning. Quinn blew out a big breath and followed Clay to the sanctuary.

Quinn parked in an empty spot in front of Clay's ranch house. From the number of cars, he had plenty of guests. Quinn hoped for a quiet early morning walk with Lacie, but there were probably guests on all the trails. Where could he take her to talk?

He got out of the truck and jogged to the house. What was up with her anyway?

He'd waited half the evening for her to finish cleaning the church, but she'd avoided him. And it seemed purpose-

ful. Something happened last night, and he didn't have a clue what. She'd disappeared, and even her mother hadn't known when she left.

Something was wrong, and now he had to tell her the truth. He'd feel better about it, if they were on a cozier standing, like before the wedding. Her mom did say Lacie had a headache. Maybe that's all it was. He sure hoped so.

His mission weighed so heavy, he'd gotten up way too early and driven straight here. She probably wasn't even up yet. Especially if she had a headache.

He entered the ranch house. A few guests sat in the living area, and he heard voices and breakfast clatter in the kitchen. He charged up the stairs.

Why had he waited so long? If he'd told Lacie the truth back when he'd first moved to Aubrey, maybe she'd have gotten over it.

This way, he'd held out on her. If by some miracle she didn't blame him for Mel's death, she might not trust him again. His mama always told him withholding the truth was the same as lying. He'd lied to Lacie. About the most traumatic event in her life. Why should she ever trust him again?

He knocked, and heavy footfalls creaked the floor. Too heavy to be Lacie's. His heart sank lower. Another man? No, what was he thinking? Things had gotten pretty intense between them lately, but she wasn't the type of woman to let any man spend the night unless he put a ring on her finger.

Worrying about his secret was messing with his head.

The door opened. Her dad. Duh.

"Morning." Her dad held a piece of paper. "I was trying to find Lacie. Thought since it was her place, I shouldn't be answering the door. But she's not here. Found this on her pillow."

Quinn took the note and read it: *Don't worry. Just need time to think.*

"You don't have any idea where she went or when she'll be back?"

"Nope. We're just clearing out. It was real late when we left the church last night, so we crashed here. Was she expecting you?"

Words stuck in his throat. He nodded. We were supposed to spend the day together. *I was supposed to crush her heart and any love she ever had for me.*

"I'll tell her you stopped by."

"Thanks. Have her call me as soon as she gets back." He trudged down the stairs. Her SUV was here. She was either at Rayna's or walking somewhere on the ranch. Like a needle in a haystack. Or along with dozens of other dude ranch guests.

He eased his truck out of the lot and into Clay's driveway. Clay was always up early. As he neared the house, he could see Clay and Rayna on the front-porch swing.

"Morning," Rayna called. "What brings you around so early?"

"Have y'all seen Lacie?"

"Not since last night. She's probably not even up yet."

"I went to the house. She's not there."

Clay sat silent.

Had he told her? A slow boil burned in Quinn's chest. He stomped up on the porch. "You didn't—"

"I told you I wouldn't, and I didn't."

"What's going on here?" Rayna frowned.

Quinn counted to ten. "Sorry. I'm just worried." And in torment. "I really need to talk to her."

"We'll tell her you stopped by."

"Sorry to interrupt your morning." He hurried down the steps and stopped. "I really do love her."

"I know," Clay admitted. "You might check the stalls. See if Copper's around. You can borrow one of my horses if you need to. That is, if you calm it down first."

"Thanks." Why didn't he think of that? Because he was past thinking at this point. He vaulted to the barn.

* * *

Lacie sat against the trunk of a huge weeping willow tree. The feathery, droopy leaves hung almost to the ground in places. She clutched her pocketsize Bible to her heart after reading the same passage five times.

She'd held Max half the night, prayed and thought, instead of sleeping. Her ears rang with lack of sleep, but she was still wide-eyed. She'd decided one thing—contact Star about finding a house for her and Max. Somewhere on the outskirts of Aubrey, near Denton. Farther away from Quinn and his lies.

Her cell rang, and Copper's ears twitched.

"Where are you?" Rayna didn't even give her a chance to say hello.

"On the west trail. I rode Copper out."

"I don't know what's going on. Quinn was just here—he and Clay are acting weird. And I think Quinn's riding out to find you."

Her phone beeped with another call. She pulled it away to look. Quinn's number, sure enough. "He's calling me now."

"You gonna answer?"

"Thanks for calling me."

"I don't know what's up, but he loves you. He looks like he's in agony just because he can't find you. I sure hope you can work it out with him."

Lacie's mouth opened then clamped shut. She hung up. Quinn would head down the main trail. Maybe she could beat him back to the barn and put Copper up. But then what?

She mounted Copper and reined her into the brush, deeper and deeper, until Lacie couldn't see the trail anymore. Copper flinched as tree branches clawed at them, and twigs cracked under her hooves. "Easy, girl."

Copper whirled back toward the trail and bolted for it.

"*Whoa*, Copper. *Whoa*." Lacie dodged tree limbs.

Copper made it back to the trail and stopped dead.

Lacie nearly went over the saddle horn, but she hung on. "Sorry, girl. I forgot you're not an off-the-trail sort of gal."

Hoof beats sounded from behind.

She caught a glimpse of Quinn. "*Yah!*"

Copper took off again, charging down the trail.

"Lacie, wait up. It's me."

She ran Copper harder.

"Lacie, why are you running from me?"

Why was she? If she outran him, he'd only catch up with her later. End this now.

"Whoa." She pulled on Copper's reins. At full throttle, it took a few yards for her horse to stop.

Chapter 18

"Good girl." Lacie patted Copper's rust-colored shoulder and turned to face Quinn.

His horse stopped near hers. "Why are you running from me?"

Worry etched lines around his eyes. But she couldn't be taken in by him. Not again.

"I didn't know you were there." The lie came out too easy. Served him right. He wasn't the only one who could hide the truth.

Quinn swung down off his horse. "We have to talk."

"Now isn't a good time."

"It has to be. Let me help you down."

"I'm fine right here."

He frowned. "Is something wrong?"

A bitter laugh escaped. It didn't sound like anything that had ever come out of her mouth. "Everything is wrong."

"Why?"

"Because I know what you have to tell me."

"No, you don't. You can't possibly imagine."

"You raised Cactus Red."

His jaw clenched. "Clay told you."

"No." Tears stung all the way down to her throat. "I overheard you telling him at the church last night."

Quinn closed his eyes. "Lacie, please come down here so we can talk."

"Oh—now you want to talk." Sarcasm coated her tone. "Don't you think it's just a little late?"

"I wanted to tell you."

"But you didn't. For six whole months. And all that time, you wormed."

"For a long time, I blamed myself for Mel's death. I was afraid if I told you, you'd blame me, too. And hate me. I love you, Lacie."

"No. You don't. You know everything about me. But I wonder what else have you held back? Love is about honesty. And obviously, you don't know how to be honest." Her heels sank into Copper's sides, and the horse shot off like a rocket. *Eat my dust, Quinn.* Hysterical laughter bubbled up her throat, followed by hot, blinding tears.

Lacie stared out the window of Rayna's kitchen. Oh Lord, Quinn had almost been perfect. If only he'd been honest with her.

"Earth to Lacie." Rayna waved her hand at her. "Maybe my news will cheer you up. Kendra is pregnant."

Lacie placed a hand on her stomach. "I'm so happy for them. A baby." It seemed like only yesterday she'd been pregnant with Max.

"I think everything's working out for them." Rayna refilled their tea glasses. "Kendra's feeling better about Danielle since Lynn and Trent are both in college. I invited Kendra to join us, but she's having morning sickness well into the afternoon. Thank goodness I never had that."

Kayla and Max played, content in the corner surrounded by toys. Gibberish, mixed with authentic words, filled Rayna's kitchen.

"I didn't, either. My last months' were stressed and sad, but still happy."

"You were such a trooper."

"It comforted me to know I'd have a child to remember Mel by. Sometimes, I wonder what it would have been like if we'd had Max earlier. Back when Mel wanted to have a baby, but I wouldn't because I was afraid something would happen to him." The irony tasted bitter.

Everything she'd wanted had been within her grasp. But then he died.

Countless, sleepless nights had plagued her afterward. If she hadn't pulled his strings, would he still be here with her? Clay had told her Mel looked forward to quitting, and she knew God was in control of life and death. But still, she wondered.

She'd never admitted what she'd done to anyone. Not even to Mel.

And definitely not to Quinn.

Her breath stalled. She hadn't told Quinn everything. Not the scheming part.

She'd lied to him just as he'd lied to her.

And their lies had imprisoned them both.

"Lacie? Calling Lacie?" Rayna's voice broke through the fog.

She focused on her friend. "*Hmm?*"

"You were miles away. You okay?"

Max giggled, and she watched him crash his toy truck into Kayla's plastic horse.

"Could you keep Max for a little while? I need to run an errand. I'll be back before his nap time."

"Sure. Take your time."

* * *

Quinn picked up the phone. He really needed to make a few business calls. But his heart wasn't in it. His heart was dead.

Gravel crunched in his drive. He set the handset down. Wasn't expecting anybody. He peeked out the window.

Lacie's SUV? It couldn't be.

But it was.

She killed her engine, flung the door open, and vaulted to the house.

He bolted for the door and tore it open.

Her fist, poised to knock.

"Lacie?" What good sense he had left kept him from scooping her up and never letting her go.

"Can I come in?"

"Sure." He stepped aside. "It's good to see you, even though I don't deserve the privilege."

She stopped inside the doorway. "I'm not angry with you anymore."

"You're not?"

"I have something to tell you. Something I've never told anyone. Not even Mel."

"Have a seat." He tried to calm his revving heart, but it was no use. "Want some tea?"

"No, I'm fine. But I can't sit." She wrung her hands and paced across his living room. "When I was married to Mel, I wanted a baby. Really badly. He wanted to start a family, too. But the rodeo is so dangerous, I put off getting pregnant because I was afraid. We argued a lot about it. In fact, it was our only argument."

"Until he decided to quit?" His legs would surely give out, just from her nearness. He sank to the couch.

She took a deep breath. "I was tired of traveling and didn't want to wait any more for a baby. Mel was feeling all the jolts and falls more than he used to, and I didn't want him to be

too bunged up to play with our child." Her voice shook. "So I got pregnant."

"It was what you both wanted." He didn't want to think about her intimacies with her husband. "I'm sure he was very happy."

"You don't understand. I didn't tell him I'd changed my mind about having a baby. I got pregnant on purpose."

"It's not like you tricked him into becoming a daddy. He wanted it, too."

She sat down beside him. "I got pregnant so he'd quit the rodeo. I conned him into doing exactly what I wanted. And it worked. But then he died. And I've wondered ever since." Her tone reached a high-pitched squeak. "Was he distracted on that last ride? Because he didn't want to quit, but I forced him into it? It wasn't your horse that killed Mel. It was me."

"Oh, Lacie." He pulled her into his arms, unable to stay at a distance any longer.

She clung to him. "I don't really believe that. I know God is in control. We all have a time to die, and it was Mel's time. But were his last months conflicted because of me?"

"He loved you, and you were carrying his child. I'm certain his last months were happy because of that." *It would make my days.*

"I hope so." She sniffled and pulled away. "I had to tell you what I did."

"Why?"

"Because, the other day, I blasted you for not being honest with me when I hadn't been completely honest with you." She swiped at her eyes. "My deception makes me feel ugly and not worthy to be loved. It made me realize you probably didn't tell me about Cactus Red because it made you feel ugly and unworthy of love."

"You got that right." Quinn's shoulders slumped. "But what you did pales in comparison with me withholding the truth from you."

"Not really. I withheld the truth from Mel. Were you there the night he died?"

Her question knocked the wind out of him. For a moment, he couldn't breathe.

"No. I was announcing another rodeo, but the mind can do terrible things. I've had nightmares about witnessing his fall. His death."

"Me, too."

"But you were there. Even without being there, I couldn't get past it. I tried getting drunk." Tried one-night stands he couldn't go through with, and when he woke up the next morning, Mel was still dead. "I sold my business and turned to raising quarter horses. I quit announcing until Cowtown management called me."

"Going to the rodeo always made me feel closer to Mel."

"I took the Cowtown gig 'cause I thought if I got some fresh rodeo images in my head, it might get rid of the nightmares."

"Did it work?"

"They're better."

"You must have been tortured since you reconnected with me." Her soft hand cupped his cheek. "Trying to handle it on your own. Maybe we can dust off the ashes of that night together."

He quaked at her touch. Couldn't they stop talking, so he could kiss her now?

But he had to tell her all of it. "I moved to Aubrey because I knew his widow and best friend lived here. I planned to get to know them, be neighborly, and help in any way I could. I guess I thought it might ease my conscience. But I didn't know Mel's widow was you. Not until we ran into each other in that bar in Fort Worth."

"I don't blame you for his death. I hope you don't blame yourself."

Quinn closed his eyes. "I did. For a long time. Until Hank died and I got back in church. But I still should've told you."

"I understand why you didn't."

"Basically, I was afraid you'd never love me. And I couldn't deal with that."

She took both his hands in hers. "But I do love you. And I'm sorry if I hurt you."

"Oh, baby, you didn't hurt me near like I hurt you. And I deserved it. I don't deserve your love."

"Yes, you do." Her fingertips traced his jaw. "Quinn Remington, are you gonna ask me to marry you, or am I gonna have to ask you?"

"I never got around to getting a ring." He shot her a sheepish grin.

"I don't have to have a ring, not until the wedding, at least."

"Do you think we can build a happily-ever-after? Together?"

"I do."

He slid off the couch and knelt at her feet. "I wanna hear you say that in our wedding vows. Lacie Maxwell Gentry, will you marry me?"

Her arms wound around his neck, and she kissed him to within an inch of his life.

When she let go, his breathing was ragged. "Can I take that as a yes?"

"I'd never kiss a man like that unless I planned to marry him."

"Soon?"

"Definitely."

Hay bales formed makeshift pews in the clearing in the woods behind Quinn's ranch. A white lace runner covered the carpet of spring wildflowers to form an aisle between the rows of bales. Lacie stood with her father behind the guests.

Rayna and Kendra guided Max and Kayla down the long aisle. Kayla's ivory rose petals fell in clumps along the way.

Lacie's gaze riveted to Quinn at the end of the long aisle. A heart-shaped archway woven with ivy and aqua carnations framed him and Brother Timothy. Clay, Stetson, and Trent stood at Quinn's side.

The casual setting fit her and Quinn. Her aqua-carnation and ivory-rose bouquet went nicely with her rhinestone-embellished denim skirt, cowgirl boots, and crisp white blouse, lined with more rhinestones. She wore her turquoise jewelry that Quinn liked.

After their ceremony, they'd ride Quinn's horse into the sunset and end up at Trent's old cabin for their honeymoon night. Lacie shivered with anticipation.

Quinn wore black jeans, cowboy boots, and a celery-colored shirt, with his hat pulled low over his gorgeous eyes. One fine cowboy, and he couldn't seem to look away from her either.

Finally, Kayla ran out of petals, and Rayna hurried the children along.

The church pianist began the wedding march on her portable keyboard, and Lacie had to concentrate to keep her slow, stutter-step pace, when all she wanted was to run at full tilt and leap into Quinn's arms.

God was so good. Twice, he'd given her a godly man who loved her to pieces. How could one woman be so blessed?

Yes, part of their hearts had died with Mel that night. But God led them to each other and gave them strength to rise from the rodeo ashes and find happily-ever-after. Together.

Thank You, Lord, for letting him worm his way into my reawakened heart.

Max escaped Rayna and hurled himself at Quinn. Rayna scurried to catch him, but Quinn scooped him up.

"Howdy, little partner." Quinn kissed Max's temple.

Now, only a few feet away from her husband to be, she dashed toward him.

Quinn's arms came around her, and Max wriggled between them.

Her heart filled to overflowing.

Laughter swept over their guests.

Brother Timothy cleared his throat. "Should I skip to the end?"

"No." Quinn's lips brushed her ear. "I've been worming—I mean—waiting to marry this woman for ten years. Give us the works."

Lacie pulled away just far enough to get lost in Quinn's eyes. In their celery-colored depths she could see her past and her future. And their future shone with a brilliant rhinestone shimmer.

* * * * *

REQUEST YOUR FREE BOOKS!

2 FREE INSPIRATIONAL NOVELS
PLUS 2
FREE
MYSTERY GIFTS

Love Inspired

SHANNON TAYLOR VANNATTER

is a stay-at-home mom/pastor's wife/writer. When not writing, she runs circles in the care and feeding of her husband, Grant, their son, and their church congregation. Home is a central Arkansas zoo with two charcoal-gray cats, a chocolate Lab, and three dachshunds in weenie dog heaven. If given the chance to clean house or write, she'd rather write. Her goal is to hire Alice from *The Brady Bunch*.

Books by Shannon Taylor Vannatter

HEARTSONG PRESENTS

HP902—*White Roses*
HP921—*White Doves*
HP937—*White Pearls*
HP974—*Rodeo Dust*
HP997—*Rodeo Hero*

**Lacie's breath caught. *Step back.
Run for the house.* Her eyes closed.**

Quinn's lips touched hers. A whisper of a kiss. His arms came around her, pulling her close.

Her palms rested on his chest. His heart beat steady under her fingertips. Her hands moved up his shoulders and curved around his neck.

The kiss deepened. His lips tasted hers, soft, tender, yielding. His breathing ragged.

He pulled away, stiffened, and set her away from him. "I'm sorry—I shouldn't have done that. But I've wanted to for almost ten years. I'm sorry."

Lacie spun away from him and ran. Darkness had fallen like a curtain. Blindly, frantically, she managed to find her SUV in the glow of the porch light. As she tore out of the drive, she risked a glance at the barn. She could barely make out Quinn's dark shape in the doorway. A living, breathing man who possessed the power to steal her heart from Mel. The only man she'd ever pledged it to—until death did they part.